Mehsia's Medallion

Gangsta Medieval

Brenda Walker

WALKER PRESS, INC.

This novel is a work of fiction. All of the names, characters, places and incidents either are the product of the author's imagination or are used fictitiously. Any resemblance to actual persons, living or dead, events, or locales, is entirely coincidental.

CONTENTS

ACKNOWLEDGEMENTS

To my readers, family, friends, who have waited patiently for me to complete this novel, I salute you for your love, encouragement, and support. I've had so much fun creating characters and writing this story using my newly created writing style known as *"Gangsta medieval."* Gangsta Medieval storytelling is a unique combination of medieval, gothic with an urban attitude. It's funny, dramatic, suspenseful and exciting. So enjoy!

But before you get started, there are a few people I would like to thank, Ms. Carla Kinslow for being my Best Friend Forever - BFF. Special thanks to Dr. Ervin "Ray" Deloney, D.O. for all his encouragement and support. Thanks, to Terri Thomas for keeping it real and keeping me laughing. To Maya Arie O'Connor, Grannies' Baby, I love you with all my heart and I hope you are inspired to write a novel someday. I would like to personally thank my Lord and Savior, for loving me unconditionally.

PROLOGUE

The smell of death filled the air. Hundreds of dead bodies covered the Isle of Peoria, a small body of land nestled just twenty miles south of Mehsia. Many soldiers were dead, their body parts scattered from land to sea. The gruesome scene was the result of the latest battle between the Mehsia and Isshi armies. The unexplained growing tensions between the two kingdoms, which had begun several years before, had led to a series of bloody battles for the control over the Isle. Over the last several days, the Isshi army had conducted grueling and brutal, murderous slashing and beheading of the Mehsia soldiers. Although the Mehsia soldiers were experiencing a great defeat, the remaining warriors were determined to die with honor, vowing to fight until their deaths.

In the eastern end of the Region, King Ramnah reigned over the lands of Isshite people. It was there where he was strategically planning numerous battles to conquer the entire Region, including the western lands currently occupied by Kingdom of Mehsia.

"I shall conquer them all and rule the entire Region!" exclaimed King Ramnah.

In the western end of the Region was the Kingdom of Mehsia, which was under the rule of King Hubaka, an elderly man who had ruled over the Mehsian people for more than seventy years.

Unbeknownst to the people of Mehsia, King Hubaka was dying and his wife, Queen Jacuma, had been ruling the kingdom in support of her ailing husband. Queen Jacuma was a strong, assertive woman who refused to concede to the pressures of King Ramnah.

CHAPTER 1

Knock. Knock. "Enter, please," said the queen as she scribed a letter while sitting at the gold, oval-shaped desk in the parlor.

Queen Jacuma was the epitome of elegance with her long, silky black hair, which was always neatly pinned up with priceless golden jewels. The queen's posture was erect as she sat at the desk writing, poised just as she had been taught by her royal mentors. Her flawless caramel skin was smooth and seeped of oils and scents made from the finest, rarest, and most sensuous flora in all the lands. The artistry of bold and vibrant colors, so charily painted on her face, seemed to define her natural beauty while exuding excessive femininity. But the true essence of the queen's persona was yet to be discovered by those closest to her, and was far from the enchanting outer beauty she so graciously portrayed. Deep within her very soul lurked idiosyncrasies bewilderingly equal to the strength of a warrior in combat.

"Queen, Your Majesty, you have an urgent message from Lord Phillip, the Commissioner of the Army," said Casper politely, as he entered the parlor.

"Urgent? Is it regarding the war?" asked the queen.

"I suppose so, Your Majesty," said Casper.

"Well then, let him in, Casper. I will see him now," said the queen.

Casper quickly returned to the foyer, where Lord Phillip was waiting, and informed him that the queen would see him now. He opened the door and announced the arrival of Lord Phillip, a tall, dark, handsome warrior in a worn suit of battle armor.

"I hope you have good news, my lord," said the queen sharply. She laid down her writing pen and turned toward the two gentlemen, implying that she was giving this matter her undivided attention.

Lord Phillip kneeled down on one knee and kissed her ring. "It is always a pleasure to see you, my beautiful queen," he said.

"Oh Phillip, spare me the gibberish! Are the men okay?" asked the queen hastily.

"No, Your Majesty. Unfortunately, I have troubling news. Our men, well most of our men, are dead and the remaining men, well... well, it's very bad news for Mehsia. We have been defeated by the Isshi army on the Isle of Peoria," said Lord Phillip, dropping his head in total humiliation.

Angrily, the queen commanded Casper to bring Ouray, the sorcerer.

"My queen, must you resort to such mockery and mystical garbage on such serious military matters?" said Lord Phillip as if to insinuate that the queen did not trust his judgment as the leader of the army.

The queen quickly looked over at Lord Phillip. "I suggest you watch your tongue in my presence, sir. You have no right to question my actions," she said angrily. "Those men were under your leadership, and if they have been defeated in the grueling manner you have stated, then it's a reflection of your mystical bullshit leadership abilities as Commissioner of this army."

"But my queen," said Lord Phillip harshly.

"I shall hear no more from the likes of you, sir. I trusted you with the lives of those men!" shouted the queen. She immediately turned toward Casper and gritted her teeth. "Get me Ouray. Now."

"Yes, my queen," Casper quickly replied. He turned toward Lord Phillip and smirked. "Shall I also show Lord Phillip the door, madam?"

"Yes, that would be appropriate," said the queen, returning her attention to her writings on the desk.

It had been rumored through the kingdom for years that Lord Phillip had always held a secret—but not so hidden—love for Queen Jacuma. But Casper had been serving the royal family for years and felt it was his unwritten honor to protect the king and queen from falling prey to those destined to seduce either of them into infidelity or other lustful acts outside of their marriage. In this self-bestowed role, Casper believed it was necessary to serve as a confidant and protector of the king and queen.

Lord Phillip, humiliated by the scathing remarks made by the queen and the antagonistic scoffs of Casper, stared silently at both of them for a brief minute and then abruptly exited the parlor.

CHAPTER 2

Ouray, the sorcerer, entered the parlor in a state of servitude. "My queen, what is of such urgency?" he asked snippily. "I was entertaining my fellow eunuchs from far away, so I hope it is nothing of too much concern. I must return to my frolic and fun!" he laughed.

"Ouray, I'm concerned about the war. Terrible, terrible news has reached the king's court. The men are dying and the army has been defeated by King Ramnah," replied the queen, as she purposefully sought a resolution to the war issues plaguing her mind. "You must do something. Can't you spin a spell or send some demonic forces to stop this tragedy of a war?" She threw her hands up into the air. "Oh please, Ouray. Please. You must help the king and me," she pleaded desperately. She fell to her knees like a helpless peasant girl—which was contrary to her stronger, more feminine leadership style.

Ouray, half man-half horse, had a strong, manly upper body, demonic facial features, and long silver hair that flowed as his lower stallion body moved. He looked down upon the queen, shocked by her desperate and unbecoming act, and said in a deep and profound voice, "Queen! Queen! Please, Your Highness, try and compose yourself." He sighed in disgust at the queen's helpless behavior. "What would you have me do? Or better yet, what are you willing to forsake to save your pitiful little army?" he asked devilishly.

Astonished by Ouray's remarks, the queen immediately rose to her feet. "Whatever do you mean?" She quickly regained the composure required of royalty.

"Well, I assume you realize this is a serious and complicated matter, my queen," said Ouray in a somewhat combative but respectful manner. "You see, the way I figure this is that your army has been defeated by King Ramnah. That means you lose control over Mehsia, and that you and King Hubaka will be beheaded—let's say by noon tomorrow."

"Bastard, you half beast of a man, how dare you speak death to me in such a disrespectful and ungrateful manner!" said the queen angrily. "I am your queen, and my husband has protected you and taken care of your sorry family for years. A beast like you can only dream of being a human or being able to conceive a child." Bitterly, she continued to demean and degrade the physical and inhuman characteristics and features of Ouray, knowing that such hurtful words would scar the deepest parts of his hardened soul. It was known that all eunuchs desired to conceive children like humans. As the queen slowly moved closer toward Ouray's face, stopping just inches away from his nose, she leaned forward. "I should have you burned alive for your offensive tongue."

Perilously aroused by the queen's aggressive posture, and concerned for her safety, Casper quickly drew his sword and rushed across the room toward Ouray, shouting, "Shall I take him to the courtyard for the burning, my queen?"

"You will do nothing of the sort," replied Ouray

as he rose up on his hind legs to defend himself against Casper. The two men faced off, positioning themselves for an intense and bloody battle.

"Hold on!" shouted the queen. "I will settle this matter with Ouray. Casper, please back off."

Casper slowly retreated toward the door. As he exited the room, he said to the queen, "I will be on the other side of this door, if you need me." He looked at Ouray. "As for you, this is not over."

"Yeah, back off, you half pint," said Ouray sarcastically.

Casper snarled and slammed the door as he left the room.

"Okay Ouray, let's cut to the chase. What is your price?" asked the queen assertively.

"I have no price, yet. I will take up this issue with

my mystical powers and get back to you," said Ouray.

"How much time will it take you to fix this mess?" asked the queen.

"Uh, I will have a solution by tomorrow's nightfall," said Ouray. "But one thing you must remember, my queen—King Ramnah is an arrogant and evil bastard, you know, and he will go to great measures to prove his point by seeking revenge against you and destroying this kingdom."

"What point?" asked the queen innocently.

"Don't play naïve, my queen. I do have mystical powers and I know the secrets of many people, including my dear queen and her king." Ouray slowly walked over to the queen and grabbed her chin. He turned her face toward his face while looking into her eyes. "The eyes tell the stories of the soul," he said poetically.

The queen pushed his hands away from her chin with a look filled with humility and shame, all the time wondering what, if anything, he knew about her past. Embarrassed by Ouray's remarks, she said somberly, "The king's and my secrets cannot be revealed to anyone—they would destroy this kingdom and hurt many others."

"I know the depth of your sins, my queen. The question is: do you know the depth of these sins?" said Ouray. "Despite your lingering perplexities, innocent men are dying at war; therefore, I will help you. Tomorrow's midnight, I will return with a resolution for you and King Hubaka," he said as he exited the parlor.

CHAPTER 3

Ouray and his entourage of eunuchs began their travels across the lands to the kingdom of Isshi. Although the rolling hills surrounding the region were low and dense, displaying the beautiful countryside that connected the two regions, it still remained a very difficult journey.

It was the dead of winter, and the bone-chilling cold caused several eunuchs to freeze to death, while the remaining eunuchs fed off the flesh of their frozen bodies. They took delight in preparing a fire and roasting the flesh and bones of their dead and deliciously tasty, traveling companions—at one point fighting over the meatiest parts. In the background, one could hear the sounds of flesh being pulled apart and fists being pounded into the faces of other eunuchs as the beasts fought over their deathly delicacies.

"Give it a rest, enough already!" Ouray shouted at the eunuchs who were fighting. "Here." He threw the leg and thigh he was eating over toward them. "There is plenty more where that came from." Ouray looked into the faces of the eight remaining eunuchs sitting around the fire.

Surprised by Ouray's remark, they began to look at each other very suspiciously.

Shortly after the journey to Isshi began, Lord Phillip crossed the path of Ouray and his eunuchs.

"Hello, Lord Phillip, what brings you this way?" asked Ouray.

"I'm in battle with the Isshi army and most of my men are dead," replied Lord Phillip.

"Yes, I know," said Ouray. "The queen is devastated and wants a quick and easy closure to this war."

"There is no easy resolution to this damn war," replied Lord Phillip.

"I know, that is why I'm headed to confer with King Ramnah," said Ouray.

"How dare that woman send you to resolve my war? I am the general of this army and I will fight the battles to protect our kingdom," said Lord Phillip angrily, struggling with the embarrassment of an immensely bruised ego.

"Yeah, but evidently you have gotten your ass kicked out there. I don't mean to be harsh, my lord," Ouray said apologetically. "But the flow of blood from the Isle of Peoria is from the bodies of the men of Mehsia," he said sadly. "Here, my lord, please have a seat. Let's talk."

The two men sat by the fire and began to discuss the troubled war. Lord Phillip explained to Ouray what he thought had gone wrong in his strategic war plan. He believed the war was senseless and had no idea how such a brutal war could have ever begun. What could these two kingdoms possibly be battling over?

In response, Ouray cautiously explained to Lord Phillip that the war had begun because of lies and secrets between the two kingdoms. Lord Phillip wanted to probe more about the lies and secrets, but didn't want Ouray to know how keenly interested he was in the scandals that existed between the two kingdoms. And surely, he didn't want Ouray to know he was in love with Queen Jacuma and would do anything to protect her.

"Well, we must devise a plan to prevent King Ramnah from conquering the Kingdom of Mehsia," said Ouray.

"Do you have something particular in mind?" asked Lord Phillip.

"Of course I have a plan," replied Ouray.

"Go ahead and explain it, big dummy," said Lord Phillip impatiently.

Laughing at Lord Phillip's remarks, Ouray began to explain his plan. "You see, my lord, King Ramnah has only one desire and that is to rule both the eastern and western parts of the region. Well, since he has kicked your ass on the battlefield and has conquered the Isle of Peoria, he is only days from moving his men forward and capturing Mehsia."

"Okay, let's say you're onto something here— how do we stop this take over?" asked Lord Phillip.

"We offer him the kingdom without any further bloodshed or death of his men. We offer him the kingdom through marriage."

"What an asinine idea!" shouted Lord Phillip. "I know King Ramnah would like to shag the queen, but not even the most dishonorable man would do such a thing while the King Hubaka is still alive."

"No not the queen, you damn fool. I am referring to Prince Kishan. We shall devise our plan based upon the marriage arrangement between Prince Kishan of Mehsia and Princess Celina of Isshi, the heirs to the two greatest kingdoms," said Ouray proudly. He stood up tall with his head held high, his shoulders back, and his chest full of pride for his brilliant, yet deceptive plan.

"The royal families of these two kingdoms won't agree to such a plan. Anyway Prince Kishan is, well, Prince Kishan. My sister, Zorresia, believes she should be married to Prince Kishan," said Lord Phillip sharply, as if to suggest some type of romantic bond existed between the two.

"Are you serious? That fat angry cow who eats all day?" Ouray laughed loudly. "She'd have better odds marrying one of my eunuchs!"

"You watch your mouth, Ouray. That angry fat cow you are referring to is my sister, you bastard," spat Lord Phillip, not realizing he'd just used the same derogatory name to refer to Lady Zorresia as had Ouray.

"Okay, I apologize," said Ouray. "But you have got to be kidding me. Prince Kishan is not her type. You know she deserves someone who would love her—I mean all of her." He gestured with his hands a big circle, symbolizing Lady Zorresia as obese in appearance. "Just think, Lord Phillip," said Ouray, "if you and I pull this off, then you could become the general of both armies and, well, I could continue to mesmerize both kingdoms with my impeccable sorcery skill and smoke my special cigars. This war would be over and there would be no more deaths." Ouray then laid back on the ground and lit his special cigar and puffed away.

"What about the queen and king of Mehsia? What would happen to them," asked Lord Phillip.

"What about them?" said Ouray uncaringly. "We would agree that they remain in the new kingdom's court as royalty. Anyway, that old bastard will be dead in a couple of months and you will get your second wish, too."

"And what wish might that be?" asked Lord Phillip.

"What? You think I don't know that you are hopelessly in love with the almighty queen of Mehsia?" replied Ouray.

"I-I don't know what you are talking about," said Lord Phillip, blushing.

"Oh don't give me that shit, my lord. I see how you look at her, how you lust for her firm breast and the sweet taste of her lips—both pairs, might I add?" Ouray laughed.

"I'm warning you, Ouray, you'd better hold your tongue," threatened Lord Phillip.

"Okay, okay, eat up and rest. Tomorrow, we'll complete our journey to Isshi to see King Ramnah," said Ouray, backing down. "I hope you will be joining me on the journey," asked Ouray.

Lord Phillip didn't answer Ouray. He laid down but didn't immediately fall asleep. He rested quietly beside Ouray and the others, thinking all the while about how they would convince King Ramnah to stop the war—just by offering Prince Kishan for marriage. What a stupid plan, he thought. What's in it for King Ramnah? Why would the King of Isshi ever agree to such a thing?

CHAPTER 4

The next morning, the weather was much warmer, and Ouray and his entourage gained many travel miles, arriving in Isshi around nine o'clock. Isshi was a beautiful kingdom filled with tradition and historic treasures. But the Isshi people were more liberal than their long time rivals—the Mehsians. The royal families and their courtiers enjoyed with the more sinful pleasures in life.

As the men arrived, the townsfolk were already rejoicing in the streets, celebrating the victories of the Isshi army on the Isle of Peoria. "Isshi! Isshi! Land of the victory!" they chanted.

"Would you like to buy some ladies' company, sirs?" said a local beggar, in a very high-pitched voice, who was wearing dirty and soiled clothing. "We have all kinds of shapes and sizes to meet your special pleasures, sirs."

"No thanks," replied Lord Phillip.

"Speak for yourself," said Ouray. "I have a little itch that needs some scratching. My sexual drive is much more stronger than you mortal humans."

"I didn't come here for that," said Lord Phillip. "We must see King Ramnah; my men's lives depend on it."

"Okay, already. Hey beggar, I'll take a rain check, but can you tell me where the king's palace is?" asked Ouray.

"Just over yonder, past the trees of passion," said the beggar.

"Thanks," replied Ouray.

The men traveled a short distance and arrived at the king's palace where they were greeted by the palace guardsmen.

"I have come to see King Ramnah," said Ouray.

"What matters could you possibly have with our king? You're half-man, half horse," laughed the guardsman.

"I want to tell the king that I am your dad-tay, you ugly trowl," Ouray replied childishly.

Angered, the guardsman drew his sword and

swung it at Ouray. Ouray disappeared and reappeared behind the guardsman and struck him over the head with his fist. The guardsman fell to the ground. The other guardsmen drew their weapons and charged toward Ouray.

"Stop it! Hold your guard!" shouted King Ramnah. "What matter brings you from far across the country to Isshi, my friend?"

"It surely wasn't to get sliced up by your guardsmen, my ole friend," said Ouray.

"Come, please come in, my friend." King Ramnah welcomed Ouray and Lord Phillip into the palace.

"I apologize for my guardsmen's behavior," said King Ramnah. "How can I help you, Ouray? But before you reply, please introduce me to your traveling companion."

"I am Lord Phillip, Your Majesty."

"Welcome to my kingdom," said King Ramnah.

"As I was saying, Lord Phillip and I have traveled a long way to see you, Your Majesty."

"Ouray, please call me Ramnah. You are no stranger to this family," said King Ramnah.

Humbled by the king's informality, Ouray relaxed and took a seat in the parlor next to the king, taking full advantage of his implied friendship with the king.

"Well, I guess by now you have heard of my victory on Isle of Peoria," said the king.

"Yes, Ramnah, I have heard of your victories, and that is the reason for my visit," said Ouray. "I would like to talk with you about the kingdom of Mehsia and the brutal slaughtering your army has inflicted upon those poor men."

"Well maybe I spoke to soon regarding informality with you," defensively replied the king. "I thought you, as my friend, would be pleased with my victories over the Mehsians."

"Unfortunately, my king, I have come in the name of the Queen Jacuma of Mehsia," said Ouray.

Surprised by these remarks, King Ramnah stood up and distanced himself from Ouray.

"Queen Jacuma would like to spare the lives of the remaining men and, of course, her life and that of King Hubaka as well." Noticing the king's reaction to his representation of Queen Jacuma and to mitigate the king's fears, Ouray continued, "Are you interested in hearing her offer?"

"Maybe. Keep talking," said King Ramnah, urging Ouray to continue with a gesture of his hand.

Ouray, believing this a positive reaction, smiled. "Well King Hubaka and his lovely wife, Queen Jacuma, are willing to make you a deal to end the war." Ouray paused to clear his throat, then he continued. "The queen is proposing a marriage arrangement between your eldest daughter and Prince Kishan, the heir to the throne of Mehsia—in exchange for your promise to end the war."

"Queen Jacuma is proposing marriage for my daughter, Celina? Has the queen lost all her senses?" asked King Ramnah, confused. "My Celina is beautiful, pure, and loving. Why on earth would I allow such a thing?" he said angrily. "I have already conquered their army and I plan to publically behead every member of their royal family, including the Prince."

"I understand that your daughter desires to be married and she is worthy of the best. Prince Kishan has been raised well by his parents, is well educated, handsome, and worth keeping alive," said Ouray. "And most importantly, he is the heir to the throne of Mehsia, the land by which you would like to rule."

"What good is it for me that my daughter should marry Prince Kishan?" asked King Ramnah. "She will become his wife and he will rule in his house. A man must rule over his kingdom and his wife."

"Yes, King Ramnah, a man must rule over his house, land, and wife, but a woman is a man's most precious jewel," said Ouray. "His home is only happy if his wife is happy. Celina could work with you to control Prince Kishan." Ouray lifted an eyebrow, like a sly cat. "In other words, my king, you could indirectly rule over Mehsia through Celina, resulting in a win-win for everyone. The princess would get a husband and you would rule both kingdoms"

"Or I could continue slaying those men and win the war—a win for my ego and a win for my kingdom—another win-win," said King Ramnah. "Ouray, let me think it over."

"King, don't wait too long; the men are dying," said Ouray. "Also, many single women are waiting to be the wife of Prince Kishan. He's truly a ladies' man. Attracts the young maidens like flies on honey."

"I agree with Ouray," said Lord Phillip, who had sat quietly during the meeting. "Prince Kishan is a fine young man and warrior."

"Okay, I get the message. I will let you know tomorrow. But for now, I will have my servants prepare for your overnight stay at the palace," replied the king. The next morning, the king rose early and spent time strategically thinking about his previous conversations with Ouray and Lord Phillip.

"Good morning, Your Highness," said Ouray.

"Good it is, indeed," replied the king. "Please sit; join me for breakfast." King Ramnah was in great spirits and eager to discuss the proposal. "Ouray, I was thinking about the proposal from Queen Jacuma. I think it is missing one valuable component," he said slyly. "I would agree to the marriage of my daughter to Prince Kishan under only one condition."

"And, what might this condition be?" Ouray asked.

"I would agree to stopping the war and to the marriage of Celina to Kishan, in return for the sacred and powerful Mehsia Medallion."

Shocked by the king's demands, Lord Phillip

choked on his bagel and spat out his drink. The liquid splashed into the face of Ouray who was sitting across the table from him.

"Is there a problem sir? Are you not well this morning?" King Ramnah asked Lord Phillip.

"Uh, no Your Majesty," muttered Lord Phillip. "It's just that no one has ever demanded the most valuable treasure in our kingdom. If the royal family surrenders the Mehsia Medallion, then you will control both the eastern and western lands and possess the utmost mystical powers. That is just too much power for one person."

"Your point is well taken, sir," replied King Ramnah cunningly. "Well, my friends, that is my final offer."

Ouray immediately agreed. "I will let the queen

know your reply. So men, it is a great day. We have an agreement and the king's word to end the brutal war," continued Ouray-with a very deceitful smirk on his face.

"Of course you have my word. What value is a man if you can't trust his words?" said King Ramnah. "The question is: will the queen keep her word? And, by the way, this deal includes your word as well, Lord Phillip. We must all agree." King Ramnah stared suspiciously at Lord Phillip.

The three men shook hands to seal the deal.

"Oh yeah, one more thing, my lord," said Ouray. "As a part of the deal the king and queen of Mehsia must remain alive and serve in the royal court."

"No problem. It would be a pleasure for them to serve me," replied the king.

"Good morning, Father."

"Good morning, Celina, it is always a pleasant surprise to behold your beauty," replied King Ramnah. "Everyone, this is my precious Princess Celina."

Ouray and Lord Phillip bowed their heads in respect while Princess Celina extended her hand.

Ouray accepted her hand and kissed it. "A pleasure indeed to behold such young and innocent beauty," he said lustfully.

"I second that," said Lord Phillip as he kissed her hand. Both men continued to extend their compliments and pleasantries to Princess Celina.

"We must prepare for our return to Mehsia," said Lord Phillip. "It was my pleasure, King Ramnah."

"Well King Ramnah, Lord Phillip and I will be on our way to Mehsia," said Ouray.

"Thank you, sirs," said King Ramnah.

The men gathered their cloaks and departed.

"Father, what business do you have with these strange men?" asked Princess Celina.

"Oh, my precious, don't worry your pretty little head with such kingdom matters," said the king. "I want you to concentrate on pampering yourself for some worthy prince to call upon you."

"Oh Father, do you ever think that will happen to me? I can only hope for the day a gentleman pursues me. It will be so romantic," said Princess Celina, as her eyes twinkled with the desires of love.

"Yes, my dear, you are beautiful, loving, and a splitting image of your handsome father. What more would a man want?" King Ramnah said jokingly.

They both laughed, and then Princess Celina said, "Oh Father, I just love your sense of humor, but most importantly, I love you."

"I love you more, princess. Now let's eat breakfast—I'm starving," said King Ramnah.

CHAPTER 5

Ouray's entourage and Lord Phillip began their journey back to Mehsia. After several hours of traveling in deep thought and silence, the men became tired. Lord Phillip suggested that the entourage rest during the night and resume their travels at daylight. They all agreed.

Suddenly, Lord Phillip broke the silence. "Ouray, do you really expect our queen and king to accept this deal? "I don't think they have a choice," replied Ouray. "As for now, the kingdom of Mehsia has lost control of the war. I know it is hard to believe, but there is something in the deal for everyone. For example, maybe King Ramnah might let you lead and command both armies. He seems pretty impressed with you."

"I know that might be a possibility, but I'm more concerned about the queen and king of Mehsia," replied Lord Phillip.

"Don't fool yourself, my lord. Like me, you care nothing about the king. You're in love with the queen," said Ouray.

"You know nothing of the sort! My concerns are regarding the possession of the Mehsia Medallion," said Lord Phillip.

The Mehsia Medallion is the Holy Grail for the kingdom. It had been passed down through hundreds of generations to the male heirs of the Mehsia kingdom.

Many stories had been told that the sacred medallion have magical powers, which are activated when the spirit of the leader meshes with the lunar position of the medallion. The mystical powers, unfettered by the medallion or whoever will possess it, could be used to create intellectual aptitudes far superior to those of normal humans. But, if the medallion were used for evil, then the power unleashed could destroy the universe, or even worse, create human forms with destructive aptitudes.

"If the medallion falls into the wrong hands, it could be used to destroy both kingdoms," said Lord Phillip.

"I know how powerful this medallion is, but we have already made a deal with King Ramnah. You worry too much. It will all work out. Let us rest now; we have a long journey ahead in the morning," said Ouray.

Lord Phillip turned over and put out his lantern, and both men fell asleep.

Ouray and Lord Phillip arrived at the Mehsia royal palace late the next evening, slightly fatigued from the long journey from Isshi, but determined to settle the deal between Queen Jacuma and King Ramnah.

"I would like to see the queen," said Ouray as he approached the palace entry gates.

"The queen is dinning with dignitaries," said Casper.

"Please interrupt, half-pint. My conversations are urgent," replied Ouray.

"I will return shortly," said Casper. He then slammed the palace door in the faces of Ouray and Lord Phillip.

"If I were not a gentleman, I would punch him in the face, dig out his eyeballs and feed them to the pigeons," said Ouray to Lord Phillip as they patiently waited outside the main door of the palace.

"Well, the way I see it Ouray, you are not a gentlemen, you're half beast. Therefore, you have all rights to sock that nitwit in the face." They laughed.

Upon returning, Casper opened the door, and surely as Ouray had just stated, he drew back his fist and punched Casper in the nose. Blood squirted everywhere.

Casper held his nose, trying to stop the bleeding and yelled, "You bastard, I will have your head for this!" The men pushed him aside and hastily made their way into the parlor to await the queen.

After about fifteen minutes the queen entered the parlor. "Ouray, I hope you bring good news," she said.

"Well, Your Majesty, some good and some not so good," replied Ouray. "King Ramnah has agreed to stop the war and spare your and the king's lives—under one major condition." He sighed. "King Ramnah wants the Mehsia Medallion."

"Is he out of his mind?" shouted the queen. "No! No! Absolutely not! Turning the medallion over to King Ramnah would destroy this kingdom and send my husband to an early grave."

"I know this is devastating news, my queen," said Ouray. "But please remember, you don't have any other choice. Either you agree to turn over the medallion to King Ramnah, or he will defeat your army, overthrowing the royal court. Kill innocent woman and children, and you and your feeble husband will be hanged. At least if you agree to the deal, you get to stay alive!"

"Are you threatening me, Ouray?" said the queen. "I have slit men's necks for less harsh words."

"May I speak sensibly?" interrupted Lord Phillip.

"Yes, you may," said the queen sharply.

Lord Phillip walked across the room to the queen and gently held her hands "My queen, I know these words might be difficult for you to accept. But King Ramnah does have us in a complicated situation. Do you think you can encourage Prince Kishan to ask the king for the medallion?"

The queen yanked her hands away from Lord Phillip and sadly looked into his eyes. "You are in on this, too, Phillip? How could you, of all people, expect me to ask my son to betray his father?"

"No my queen, not betrayal," replied Lord Phillip softly. "But, what if Prince Kishan married Princess

Celina, the eldest daughter and heir to the Isshi Kingdom? It would be a marriage arrangement, not necessarily a betrayal. Anyway, it is time for the prince to select a wife—and Princess Celina has matured into a beautiful young lady."

The queen paused in silence and sat staring into the air, looking puzzled by his suggestion that she encourage her son to marry her enemy's daughter. "It is still unclear to me why my son should marry Princess Celina," she said. "What does marriage have to do with the Mehsia Medallion?"

"Well, you could inform the king that the family is requesting the Mehsia Medallion be presented as the 'wedding dowry,'" replied Lord Phillip.

"My God, Lord Phillip, don't you think that the medallion is a very high price to pay for any young lady's hand in marriage?" replied the queen. "A couple of horses, maybe jewels, or even gold, but not the most valuable asset of this kingdom. And by the way," she continued, "everyone knows that the medallion is in a secret location known only by King Hubaka. Are there no other options?"

"Enough of this sentimental babbling. Listen to me, queen, there are no other choices!" yelled Ouray.

The queen, upset at Ouray's insensitive, harsh behavior, and feeling defeated, sat down in the chair next to the lounge in a state of dismay. As tears filled her eyes, she said in a soft and low tone, "I guess you're right, Ouray. I have no choice."

"Then it is settled. We will proceed with the terms of 'the deal,'" replied Ouray.

As the men exited the parlor, Queen Jacuma

asked that they leave through the side door to avoid being seen by her guest and King Hubaka. They left through the side door, first Lord Phillip, and then Ouray.

Bang! They heard a loud sound. Lord Phillip immediately turned around to find Ouray lying on the floor, holding his head. Casper had sought revenge against Ouray by hitting him over the head with an iron pan.

"Ha, ha, ha!" laughed Casper ferociously. "Now, that is called sweet revenge," he said as he walked away.

"Get up," laughed Lord Phillip. "He got you back, ole chum." He helped Ouray up off the floor and carried him outside the palace.

Meanwhile, the queen composed herself and returned to the dining room where her guests were enjoying the royal feast.

"Is everything all right, my love?" King Hubaka asked the queen.

"Yes, my king. Everything is beautiful," she said as she smiled at her husband.

"Will Lord Phillip be joining us for dinner?"

"No, my love; he has to rest from his long journey," replied the queen.

"Any news regarding the war?" asked the king.

The queen calmly stroked his hand. "We will talk later, my dear, but for now we must be good stewards and entertain our guest."

"Hello, Your Majesties, my name is Isabella," said a little girl with a round face and pink ribbons in her hair.

"You are a little darling," said the queen.

"Thank you, my queen. You are beautiful, too,"

replied the little girl as she stared wide-eyed at the queen. Isabella bowed her head in respect and then skipped away.

The queen sat at the dinner table, trying to maintain her eloquent and poised composure while pondering the dilemma regarding the deal. Although she was devastated, she continued to smile gracefully and even managed to laugh at every one of her guest's jokes. "I must find a way to resolve this dilemma," she thought to herself. "I have to find a way to convince King Hubaka to tell me or Prince Kishan where that damned medallion is hidden."

CHAPTER 6

"Hurry, Princess Celina! The carriage is waiting," pleaded Lady Sari. "I'm so excited, princess. I have never been to the Coliseum before. I hear it is beautiful." She rattled off her thoughts without taking a breath.

"Okay, Sari, I'm coming. I must get my hair just right," said Princess Celina as she primped and combed. "You must always try to look your very best at these events, because you never know what royal prince might be present."

"Oh, Celina, you are beautiful. Any prince would be happy just to be in your presence," said Lady Sari.

Princess Celina smiled and kissed Lady Sari on her forehead. She turned and looked into the mirror and said, "Perfect, utterly perfect."

The two ladies hurried down the staircase, out of the house, and into the carriage.

"What took you so long? I know, you were looking in the mirror," said Countess Tierra sharply.

"Must you be so critical of your sister, Tierra?" said Queen Mayora.

Ignoring her sister's remarks, Princess Celina pulled her mirror out of her handbag. "Jealousy is not becoming of a countess," she said finally.

"Jealousy? Why I never!" said Princess Tierra, turning her head and looking out the window of the carriage.

After several hours, the carriage approached the coliseum, Lady Sari said, "Oh, it is beautiful." The coliseum's décor was rich with royal heritage and ancient culture from various kingdoms.

The carriage pulled up in front of the entrance, which was reserved for the royal aristocrats of the surrounding kingdoms. The horseman opened the carriage door, then King Ramnah, accompanied by four beautiful ladies, got out of the carriage. They walked toward the hallway, which was laced with tall columns, spiraling fresh ivy and jasmine. It led directly to the amphitheatre, which was huge with many rows of seats angled toward the center stage. Red drapes served as the backdrop all the way around the balcony.

"Where are our seats?" asked Lady Sari anxiously. "There are so many people here, Mother.

Do you think we will find out seats before the festivities begin?"

"Excuse me, will you please assist my royal family with finding our seats?" King Ramnah asked the usher.

The young boy bowed his head to the king. "Yes, Your Majesty."

King Ramnah and the four ladies followed the usher to their seats. King Ramnah tipped the usher with a gold coin.

"Wow! Thank you, sir," said the usher.

Every year, the coliseum hosted festivities for the Warrior Festival, where men and beasts engaged in bloody life-or-death competitions. This year, Isshi and Mehsia had competitors, and most of the coliseum was filled with supporters from both kingdoms.

"Who are those beautiful creatures sitting just ten seats away?" Prince Kishan said to his mother, Queen Jacuma.

"Those lovely young ladies are the daughters of King Ramnah, the King of Isshi."

"How stunning," said Prince Kishan.

"Yes, they are beautiful ladies," said Queen Jacuma, taking a brief look over towards the Isshi royal family. There she noticed King Ramnah in his most infamous 'ram' armor and attire. She had always admired his broad shoulders draped with a ram's fur over one shoulder. As her eyes traced every inch of his body, she admired his clothing of fine white linen and silk covering his smooth, dark skin. King Ramnah's physique was well-defined, strong, and muscular. A warm feeling ran through her body as she succumbed to images of his manhood, which was pleasing to any woman's eye. "Worshipped and praised as a strong leader, but hated as a pompous, deceitful, and arrogant man," she thought.

"Are you listening?" said Prince Kishan, interrupting his mother's fervent thoughts of King Ramnah.

"Yes, my son. Why don't you be a gentleman and go over and introduce yourself to those lovely ladies, particularly to the one in the yellow dress," said the queen, referring to Princess Celina.

"Mother, I'm much more charismatic than that. I will send Casper to announce me, first."

Prince Kishan beckoned Casper +to him and requested that he send three roses over to the three ladies.

Casper bought the roses from the vendor and went over to King Ramnah and his family.

"May I approach?" he said to King Ramnah.

"Who are you?" asked King Ramnah's guardsman.

"I am Casper, servant to the royal family of the Kingdom of Mehsia," replied Casper loudly.

"Let him through," said King Ramnah. "Why are you here?" he asked Casper.

"I have come bringing gifts for your daughters from Prince Kishan of the Kingdom of Mehsia," said Casper.

King Ramnah smiled. "Proceed with presenting your gifts."

Casper lowered his head and bowed in respect to King Ramnah. He then presented each young lady with a rose. "I give you this rose as a symbol of your beauty, from Prince Kishan heir to the Kingdom of Mehsia."

As Sari and Celina accepted the roses, they smiled with joy and smelled the flowers' fresh scent.

"Thank you, sir," said Lady Sari.

"Please send my personal thanks to Prince Kishan," said Princess Celina.

"No thanks," said Countess Tierra. "I do not favor roses. I prefer more meaningful gifts. Therefore, please send my regrets to the prince."

Casper bowed again and hurried back to report everything to Prince Kishan. "Prince, prince," he called out. "All but one accepted your gifts."

"Excuse me?" said Prince Kishan in a state of disbelief. "One of the ladies refused my offering?"

"Yes, my prince. The lady said she does not favor roses and asks that you accept her apology."

"How dare she reject my gift?" said the prince.

"Which lady?"

"The one in the blue dress," replied Casper.

Prince Kishan, astonished by the rejection, said, "Well I guess I have to take care of this myself." He headed over to the three ladies to inquire about the refusal of his gifts.

"Hello, I am Prince Kishan, Your Majesty," he said assertively to King Ramnah. "I have come to personally accept the thanks and regrets of your lovely daughters."

"Please come, nice to meet you," said King Ramnah. "Allow me to introduce you to my family. This is my wife, Queen Mayora, my daughters Princess Celina, Countess Tierra, and Lady Sari."

"It is my pleasure to meet all of you beautiful ladies," said Prince Kishan.

"Young man, that was very thoughtful of you to send over those roses," said Queen Mayora. "Your parents must be very proud of you."

"Nice to meet you," said Princess Celina in her seductive, dreamy voice.

Countess Sari sat speechless, gazing into the eyes of the Prince with her mouth wide open.

"Hello, I'm Countess Tierra. I hope I didn't offend you, but I declined the rose. Unfortunately, I do not favor roses, sir."

"No, countess, I was not offended—just curious as to why such a beautiful lady would not favor one of nature's most beautiful gifts, the rose," said Prince Kishan.

"I have very high regards for myself but roses are not on my list of preferences. I prefer more intellectual and meaningful gifts like books," said Countess Tierra.

"Well, Countess Tierra, I appreciate your honesty," replied Prince Kishan.

"Lady Sari, please snap out of it. That staring is not becoming of a lady," said Tierra.

"H-hello," stuttered Lady Sari. "N-nice to meet you, sir."

Prince Kishan blushed and gently took her hand and kissed it. Lady Sari slowly pulled back her hand as she stared into his face, memorized by his beautiful big brown eyes with long lashes. The prince was gorgeously polite and had a sensitive charm about him, which made all the ladies, both young and old, desire to be in his presence. Lady Sari looked down at her hand, then looked up at the six foot four inch, fair skinned, handsome young prince, then looked down at her hand again and vowed never to wash that particular hand again. She then reached up and gently stroked his face, carefully outlining his cheek bones and strong chin. "I have never seen such a more beautiful creature in all my life."

Prince Kishan smiled, both embarrassed and flattered by the compliments of the very young and innocent Lady Sari. "Good day, ladies," he said, before returning to his seat.

Princess Celina couldn't contain herself. She tried to turn away, but she couldn't and found herself intensely watching Prince Kishan's every movement as he walked back to his seat. She daydreamed about what it would feel like to have a handsome man such as the prince pursue her. As she sat waiting for the festivities to begin, she tried to forget the lingering smile, the beautiful eyes, and the charming persona of the handsome prince. But the thoughts of him played over and over in her mind. Princess Celina felt a warm sensation in her body and a tingling in her vaginal area that she had experienced feeling only once before with a man.

No longer able to constraint her thoughts, she whispered to Queen Mayora, "I wonder if he's spoken for?"

"I doubt it. No man who is betrothed to one woman, sends other women flowers," replied Queen Mayora softly. She was a loving wife and mother to her three daughters, and as a loving mother, she made them all feel equally special. But secretly, she had her favorite girl of her three daughters. Queen Mayora didn't leave the palace much, and King Ramnah rarely took her any place with him, unless it was a special occasion—such as the annual festival at the coliseum. Many people said that, although the queen was beautiful, soft-spoken, intelligent, and well-educated, she lacked the kind of seductive femininity that appealed to her husband. And as a result, the king wasn't proud of his wife's beauty and often engaged in numerous extramarital love affairs. But oddly, he never gave his heart to those women. Neither, did he let them disrespect his wife.

It was rumored that King Ramnah had once loved a young maiden with all his heart many years ago, but she and her family had been exiled, forbidden to ever return to the Kingdom of Isshi. Many people said that after that day, the king never seemed the same regarding his feelings for women. He had become cold-hearted and indifferent towards women. He carried, however, a noticeably strange and unusual type of love and admiration for one of his daughters—Princess Celina. 'Strange and odd' indeed described the king's bizarre love for his daughter, but no one would dare publically render their opinion of the royal family and their eccentric behaviors—in fear of being beheaded.

Suddenly, horns sounded and the lanterns exploded with fire all around the coliseum. The announcer said loudly, "Ladies and gentlemen, let the festivities begin."

Two horsemen entered the arena, each on a stallion and in full armor, with long daggers in their hands, ready for battle. They charged toward each other at full speed, trying to throw the other off his horse. The crowd cheered with enthusiasm and suspense as the men began their battle. The men repeated their attacks against each other until one of them was knocked off his horse.

The crowd stood on their feet and roared with excitement. One man yelled, "Kill him, kill the bastard!" The horsemen remounted his horse and charged toward the other warrior, this time stabbing him in the shoulder. The crowd roared in astonishment. A lady in the crowd called, "I've seen better fights between old servant women." Another person yelled, "Show me more blood, you dirty rascals!" The men continued their bloody battle in the coliseum, and the crowds of people continued to yell and cheer them on.

"Prince Kishan, Prince Kishan, over here," a female voice called out. Prince Kishan looked up and saw a full-figured young maiden adorned with excessive jewels and dramatic eye makeup, waving her hand in the air. "Oh, how awfully embarrassing," said Prince Kishan as the young maiden made a mockery of herself, trying to get his attention.

"Please acknowledge her, Prince Kishan. To ignore her is rude and unbecoming to a prince," reprimanded King Hubaka.

"Oh Father, must I acknowledge every annoying young lady who desires my attention?" replied Prince Kishan.

"My son, let me remind you that you are part of the royal family and, therefore, you belong to the people. Although she may annoy you, she is a Mehsian. Besides, I happen to think Lady Zorresia would make you a very good wife," said King Hubaka.

"Wife?" shouted Prince Kishan. "Father, I forbid it! Really, Father, look at her. I mean she is a nice girl, but how could you ever assume I would fancy the likes of Lady Zorresia?"

"The outer beauty of a woman does not always

reflect her inner beauty," King Hubaka replied. "Now, listen carefully to this wise old man. Always seek the inner beauties of a woman before you get trapped by her outer beauty. But if you can get lucky like I did with your mother, it is desirable to have both inner and outer beauty."

"Yes, Father, I shall remember your wise old tales," replied the prince.

Meanwhile, Lady Zorresia had made her way over to Prince Kishan and his family. "Hello Prince Kishan," she panted out of breath. "Did you not hear me calling out your name?"

"Hello, my lady. Are you enjoying the festivities?" Prince Kishan asked, ignoring her question.

"Yes, watching the horsemen battle is exciting, but I'm waiting for the feast after the festivities," replied Lady Zorresia.

Prince Kishan leaned toward his left and whispered into his father's ear, "She *would* be ready to eat." He turned to Lady Zorresia and said mockingly, "Yes, Lady Zorresia, I hear the feast will be plentiful. Just your luck, the feast will be filled with lots of your favorite delicacies."

"Where is your brother, Lord Phillip?" Queen Jacuma asked Lady Zorresia.

"My dear brother is sitting over there next to Ouray and his smelly entourage of eunuchs," replied Lady Zorresia, pointing toward the lower level seating in the coliseum.

Prince Kishan leaned over towards his right and whispered into his mother's ear, "Mother, must you embarrass my father by asking about another man in this presence?"

"It was an innocent inquiry and, personally, I think you're out of line to question my motives," replied the queen tersely.

"Well, I'm going to return to my seat. I came over so Prince Kishan could see my new dress," said Lady Zorresia bashfully as she twirled around like a piglet ballerina.

Prince Kishan did not respond. Suddenly, he felt a sharp pain in his right arm. Queen Jacuma was pinching his arm with her fingernails in an attempt to provoke him to compliment Lady Zorresia. "Alright, I get it!" shouted Prince Kishan. "That is a very lovely dress," he said to Lady Zorresia.

"I'm glad you like it," replied Lady Zorresia. It was no secret that Lady Zorresia had deeply loved and adored Prince Kishan ever since they were little kids. She dreamed of marrying the prince someday, and she had a reputation in the kingdom of brutally beating any female admirers whom she felt were in competition for his love. She had once beaten and cut off the hair of a young maiden who had kissed the prince. The young maiden's family requested that King Hubaka publically whip Lady Zorresia as a punishment. But the king had denied their request, stating that Lady Zorresia had been mislead regarding the maiden's upbringings and was only protecting the interest of her true love, Prince Kishan. Lady Zorresia felt special, smiling and flashing her eyelashes like a little school girl, bubbling with joy as she returned to her seat.

"You know," said Queen Jacuma to Prince Kishan as she looked on at the festivities. "I think it would be nice for you to pursue one of the beautiful daughters of

King Ramnah."

"Really now, Mother?" replied Prince Kishan.

"Yes. Really, I think it is time you got serious about your future as king of Mehsia and selecting your future queen," said Queen Jacuma.

"Whom do you recommend I select, Mother?" Prince Kishan asked wittily. "I know, Princess Celina," he quickly answered his own question before the queen could respond.

"No, not quite," said the queen. "I was thinking more of the middle daughter." Queen Jacuma was good at discerning the natures of men, including the rebellious nature of her son. She knew that, if she showed favor toward the middle daughter, the prince would reject her choice. His desire to be independent and his defiant personality would lead him to challenge his mother's wishes "I heard that the middle daughter is pretty and quite the intellectual. A great choice to replace me," exclaimed the queen.

Almost instantly, and just as the queen had predicted, the prince tersely responded, "No Mother, she's the one who rejected my rose. I would rather pursue the youngest daughter before I pursue such a high-tempered woman like Countess Tierra."

"The youngest daughter is just a kid, my dear; she hasn't even grown her breasts," laughed the queen. "Well, I guess that leaves the oldest daughter—Princess Celina. She's okay, I guess, if you like that kind of girl. Totally unlike me—all beauty and no brains."

"She comes from a royal family and happens to be the heir to the Kingdom of Isshi. Is that not worth something. Mother?" replied Prince Kishan hastily to defend the honor of Princess Celina against his mother's unpleasant comments.

"So is it your desire to someday rule both Isshi and Mehsia—the entire region?" asked the queen.

"No," replied Prince Kishan.

"Then do tell what me, my son, of what value is her lineage or the fact that she is heir to the Isshi throne to your happiness as a man?" said the queen. "None, absolutely no value."

"Okay, Mother, I have had enough of your sarcastic remarks. I want to observe the festivities," snapped Prince Kishan.

After listening to her son's overly sensitive reactions to her not-so-pleasant comments regarding Princess Celina, Queen Jacuma smiled to herself. She was confident she had manipulatively aroused emotions that had lain dormant inside the heart of Prince Kishan. As the queen sat quietly, she decided not to respond to the prince's last outburst. "Instead," she thought, "hopefully I have stirred up enough emotional interest within him that he will pursue 'the right girl' to complete 'the deal.'"

CHAPTER 7

"Princess Celina, you have a guest," the servant called up the staircase toward the princess's bedroom.

"Who might it be?" Princess Celina replied as she sat at the vanity brushing her hair. Princess Celina was the eldest and most beautiful of the three daughters of King Ramnah. Her stunning beauty surpassed that of every woman in the kingdom. She was a lightly caramel-toned and curvaceous young lady, with long, thick, curly light brown hair that lay perfectly around her face and complemented her emerald colored eyes. She was the epitome of a storybook princess.

"It is a young man, my lady. He says he is a prince," replied the servant.

"A prince? Oh my!" said Princess Celina, surprised. She hurried down the staircase toward the front door. She could see the image of a young man with curly black locks of hair standing with his back to her in the doorway.

"May I help you, sir?" she asked cautiously.

The young man turned around and Prince Celina was surprised to see he was Prince Kishan. The prince was stylishly dressed in his prestigious and colorful garments with gold and other jewels attached to his cloak.

"Hello my lady, I mean, hello Princess Celina," said the prince nervously. "I hope I'm not imposing upon you at this hour."

"No, no bother at all," replied Prince Celina. "Please do come in." She told the servant to bring refreshments into the parlor.

Prince Kishan entered the parlor and looked around. "What beautiful and distinctive décor," he said. "Full of history, ancient architectural art, and *rams*!" shouted Prince Kishan in surprise as he backed into the full-sized stuffed ram statue. The prince noticed the room was decorated with all sorts of images and statues of rams. Most notably, was and the huge ram's head stuffed and mounted over the fireplace.

Princess Celina laughed. "Oh my father, the king, is truly infatuated with the characteristics of the ram. He believes that this animal possesses godly powers and should be worshipped in his likeness. Over the past generations, my family has traveled to many foreign lands to collect these beautiful ram artifacts. But surely, Prince Kishan, you did not travel all this way to admire my father's things, did you?"

"No," responded Prince Kishan. "My princess, please sit. There is something that I would like to say. I have come to the point in my life that I, as the future king of Mehsia, must take my duty seriously. I have decided to embark on an endeavor to seek a more meaningful relationship with a lady. My princess, I have put much thought into this question. I would like to call upon you in hopes that it leads to marriage," he confessed.

Princess Celina looked into the eyes of Prince Kishan. "Yes, yes Prince Kishan!" she shouted ecstatically. "I will love to, or for us to, you know what I mean."

The two smiled and embraced each other.

"Well princess," said Prince Kishan, "I must be on my way back to Mehsia. I will return shortly to call upon you and begin our courtship."

"Yes, my prince," replied Princess Celina. Prince Kishan kissed her hand and exited the palace.

"Father, Mother, everyone, come! I have great news!" shouted Princess Celina as she twirled with excitement in the middle of the room with love and joy in her heart.

"What is all the racket about?" Queen Mayora asked as she hurried into the parlor.

"Prince Kishan has called upon me. Can you believe it, Mother? He chose me. He wants to marry me!" said Princess Celina.

"Did I hear you say that Prince Kishan asked you to marry him?" asked her mother.

"Well, what he said was that he wanted to call upon me in hopes that it would lead to marriage," replied Princess Celina, seeming less confident in her earlier statement.

"Well, that seems to be a pretty definite marriage proposal to me," said King Ramnah.

Countess Tierra and Lady Sari entered the parlor. "What is all the excitement about?" asked Lady Sari.

"Prince Kishan has just asked Princess Celina to marry him," replied King Ramnah.

"He did?" replied Lady Sari who seemed heartbroken and terribly disappointed.

"He didn't quite ask her to marry him," said Queen Mayora hoping to correct the king's misleading statement and to cast a little hope for the other sisters. "It seems he wants to start a courtship with your sister that might lead to marriage."

"Are you sure, Mother?" Sari asked.

"No, Mother is wrong, isn't she Father? The prince asked me to marry him," said Princess Celina assertively.

"Absolutely," replied the king.

Countess Tierra seemed openly irritated by the conversation. Suddenly, she lashed out bitterly at her sister. "I don't know what he sees in likes of you. You're shallow, vain, and dumb!"

"You're just jealous," cried Princess Celina. "You have always been jealous of me!"

"Oh Celina, spare me your tears. I have never been jealous of you. I believe you are a hopeless fool about love. Love is not a fairytale. Marriage is complex, hard work, and based upon unconditional love—something you could never understand. You only love yourself," said Countess Tierra bitterly.

"Now ladies," said King Ramnah. "There is no need to squabble. Princess Celina is the one that the young prince has chosen and so be it."

"Father, you always protect Princess Celina," Countess Tierra cried. "You know she's a hopeless fool about love. She has never had to sacrifice and she has always had it easy." Countess Tierra pointed toward her sister. "You only love her, Father. You love neither me nor Sari!"

"That is enough, Tierra! Go to your room, young lady," demanded King Ramnah.

Countess Tierra, was hurt by her father's harsh words. She began to cry and ran out of the parlor to her bedroom. Angered, she grabbed her cloak, climbed out the window, and sneaked out the palace.

King Ramnah immediately turned to Queen Mayora and struck her across the face with the back of his hand. "You need to teach my daughters to respect their father. I am the king of this palace."

Shamed and humiliated, Queen Mayora held her face in response to the physical abuse bestowed upon her, in front of her daughters and at the hands of their very own father. Tears filled her eyes and hatred for her husband ran rampant through the blood in her veins. Although she was in pain and a small stream of blood drizzled down her chin from the bruise on her lip, she thought, "I must hold back my tears and not let myself show weakness in front of my daughters. Her thoughts continued to plague her mind. "For if I breakdown at the hand of a man, then my daughters will forever be victims of abuse at the hand of their husbands. I won't cry," she silently repeated to herself, while sadly staring into the eyes of King Ramnah. "I will be strong."

Her bottom lip quivered as the aching pain from her wounds intensified. And for a short moment, her eyes rolled back and she was on the verge of passing out from the excruciating pain. Slowly, she was succumbing to the hurtful emotions and fears that swelled inside her. Queen Mayora could no longer hold back her tears and ran out of the parlor, holding her face.

"Go look after your mother," King Ramnah yelled to Lady Sari.

Lady Sari, frightened of her father, immediately ran out the parlor to comfort her mother.

"Now, my lovely daughter, where were we?" King Ramnah said to Princess Celina, eager to continue the excitement of the conversation despite his physical and verbal abuse against her mother and sisters.

CHAPTER 8

In good spirits, Prince Kishan arrived home from his travels to Isshi. "Well Mother, it's done," he said. "I have chosen to call upon Princess Celina for marriage."

"Did she accept, my son?"

"Of course she did. How could she resist?"

"I knew you were ready to lead this kingdom," said Queen Jacuma, as she kissed Prince Kishan on his forehead. "Well, I might be leading both kingdoms," replied Prince Kishan. "I must inform Father."

"Oh wait," said Queen Jacuma. "Maybe we should tell him later. He's resting at the moment."

"Okay Mother," said Prince Kishan, "I will tell him after dinner."

"Oh, Prince Kishan, do you mind going over to the dressmaker to pick up my fabric?" asked the queen.

"Why can't the servants do it? I am tired from traveling," said the prince.

"Because they are busy caring for your father and cleaning the palace. Surely you can do this one deed for your poor old mother," said the queen.

"Okay," replied Prince Kishan. Reluctantly, he mounted his horse and rode into town to the dressmaker's shop.

Patel was sitting in the shop's sewing room, knitting a scarf for Queen Jacuma. Suddenly, there was a knock at the door. "Who is there?" called Patel.

"It is I, Countess Tierra. Please let me in, Patel. I have much to talk with you about."

Patel opened the door and Countess Tierra ran into her arms, crying and sobbing. "Oh, Patel! Why does she have all the luck? I work so hard, I study all the time, what is wrong with me?" Countess Tierra removed her cloak and threw it on the chair.

"Who are you talking about, my dear child?" asked Patel as she picked up the cloak and neatly hung it behind the door.

"Who else? Princess Celina," whined Countess Tierra. "Prince Kishan has asked for her hand in marriage. She doesn't desire him."

"Never covet what others have, my dear," Patel responded. "What appears to be joy is not always true."

"What do you mean?" asked the countess.

"Well, Tierra, I once was in love, too, with a young man—believe it or not. But he was in love with someone else. Her name was Robecca. I used to envy her and hate her because my love, Joel, was so in love with her. I used to pray that he would see her for the Jezebel she was, leave her, and come running to me. So one day, I asked Joel to meet me at Puba's whore house in hopes that he would be able to see Robecca with other men. Once I arrived, I was surprised to see Joel engaged in uninhibited sexual activities with other men. The man whom I was hopelessly in love with didn't love me or Robecca, he liked other men. I was so embarrassed and hurt."

"But Patel," said Countess Tierra, "Prince Kishan is not that way, and Princess Celina is no Jezebel!

"I know, my dear," said Patel, "but the moral of the story is what you see on the outside of a perfect love affair is not necessarily how the people inside of the love affair really feel about each other. I found out that Joel never ever was in love with Robecca. It only seemed that way because he spent all his time with Robecca. But they both had strange sexual desires and they spent numerous hours at Puba's house to share in those experiences...with different people." Both women laughed.

"Now that's the beautiful smile I'm used to seeing," said Patel.

"Patel, whatever happened to your feelings of love for Joel?" asked Countess Tierra.

"Well, you know we became the best of friends. I used to give him pointers on how to attract men, and he used to give me pointers on how to satisfy men," replied Patel. The ladies laughed again and again.

"I guess I just have to wait to the very end of the fairytale love affair to see the real truth," said Countess Tierra.

"Yes, we will have to wait," agreed Patel. "And we must wait without injecting our own assumptions.

There came a knock at the door and a young man stuck his head through and said, "Sorry to disturb you so late, dressmaker, but Queen Jacuma has asked me to fetch her fabric."

"Oh yes, just a minute. I will prepare the queen's order. Please do come in," said Patel.

Prince Kishan entered the dressmaker's shop and stood by the counter.

"Prince Kishan, do you know Countess Tierra?"

"Yes, I had the pleasure of meeting her at the coliseum event the other day," replied the prince.

"Hello, Prince Kishan," said Countess Tierra.

"Hello," replied the prince.

"I must congratulate you on your marriage proposal to my sister, Princess Celina."

"Words surely travel fast," replied Prince Kishan. "But I guess it is in order."

"You don't sound sure of your decision," said Patel.

"Well, I do believe in love and marriage," replied the prince.

"I don't think you answered her question, Prince Kishan," said Countess Tierra.

"Countess, don't put the prince on the spot. Maybe he needs someone to talk it over with, you know, a female friend who can relate and who understands women and their needs," said Patel, as she turned and slyly looked at Countess Tierra to give her a signal.

"Oh quite surely, that would be nice. I would like to discuss everything about Princess Celina and how I could improve my courtship with her," said the prince excitedly.

Countess Tierra replied, "Well then it is done. I will tell you everything about the princess, both good and bad." The two ladies laughed.

"Okay, what's her favorite color?" asked Prince Kishan.

"Green," said Countess Tierra quickly.

"What's her favorite flower?"

"The rose," responded Tierra.

"Okay, a good start," said the prince.

"She also snores in her sleep," says the countess.

"What?" yelled the prince.

"And she rubs her ear lobe when she is nervous or lying," said the countess.

Prince Kishan stood in silence and then laughed. "I think I have enough information for now. I will be on my way. Good evening, ladies." Prince Kishan left the shop.

"Well, Patel, I feel much better. I will return home to face my troubles," said the countess.

"Ride safely, my darling," said Patel.

Tierra mounted her horse and returned to the palace.

"Hello Mother," said Countess Tierra.

"Hello, sweetheart. Why are you so cold?" Queen Mayora asked.

"I was in the horse stables," replied the countess.

"Honey, I know you are upset about Prince Kishan's proposal to your sister, but you must support her. I love you Tierra, and you are the most intellectual and educated of all my daughters," said the queen.

"I'm not as beautiful as Princess Celina. She is more shapely and prettier than I. The young lads always wanted to be with Princess Celina," said the countess in a childlike voice.

"Oh, my love, pretty she may be, but her beauty does not compare to your intellectual mind. And besides, you are more beautiful," replied the queen.

"Am I really, Mother?" asked the countess.

"Yes, my love. Yes indeed. You are my favorite girl. You're the one who really deserves the prince." The queen hugged her daughter.

Countess Tierra pulled away from her mother and looked her in the eyes, startled by her mother's remarks regarding Prince Kishan.

CHAPTER 9

It was spring time, the gardens were blooming with exotic flora, and the smell of yellow chrysanthemums filled the air around the Castle of Venothans. Lady Zorresia loved the flowers and her garden. Every morning, she delighted in prunning the unique flowers in the garden.

Lord Phillip traveled towards the Castle of Venothans. It was a place filled with memories of his mother and father and the fifteen rooms held all the family's secrets. If the walls of those rooms could speak, the tumultuous fables they would tell! But for Lord Phillip, the castle represented a sense of warmth and calmness when he came home. The castle tamed his beastly and inhumane appetite for war and killing. Lord Phillip could rely on his sister working in the garden around this time every day. As he approached the castle, he smiled. He could see Lady Zorresia in the garden. "Oh, how I love my sister," he thought.

"My brother, what brings you to the castle so early?" asked Lady Zorresia.

"My sister so lovely and full of life," said Lord Phillip as he got off his horse and kissed Lady Zorresia upon her forehead.

"I am so happy to see you, my brother," responded Lady Zorresia as she hugged her brother.

"Let's go inside. I will prepare you a meal."

"Like Mother used to make?" asked Lord Phillip happily.

"Yeah, just like Mother's," said Lady Zorresia.

The two hurried into the castle. Lady Zorresia went into the kitchen and began gathering the pots and pans to prepare the meal. She was such a good cook and had all of her mother's recipes stenciled inside her head. She gathered eggs, flour, milk, and meat. She lit the fire and heated up the water.

"I am going to freshen up a bit before my meal," said Lord Phillip. He went into his room to bathe and shave. Lord Phillip loved to sing and he exercised his vocal chords every chance he could. As he bathed and shaved, he loudly sang, "*Archery and chivalry, that is what we did, archery and chivalry, my army I have led.*"

"I see that the war has not tarnished your love for song, my brother," said Lady Zorresia as she laughed at her brother singing off-key.

"Not one bit my beloved sister, my heart continues to rejoice for song," said Lord Phillip as he sat down at the table to eat.

"I was told that a man who sings must have love in his heart. Have you found your true love, my brother?"asked Lady Zorresia inquisitively. "I know that, someday, my true love will realize the love I have in my heart for him." She remorsefully hung her head.

"Sit down, my sister. We need to have a serious talk," said Lord Phillip, as he beckoned her toward the table and pulled out a chair. "My dear sister, I must inform you of some heartbreaking news. Prince Kishan has asked Princess Celina of the kingdom of Isshi for her hand in marriage."

Lady Zorresia wailed loudly in a fanatical episode of uncontrollable crying. She shouted, "No, no! This is not happening to me! How could he love someone else? It is not true, my brother!"

"I'm afraid it is so, my sister," replied Lord Phillip.

"Brother, you must stop him. I love him! I have loved the prince ever, since we were children and over the years my love has grown so deeply for him. How could he? Oh how could he?" she cried.

Lord Phillip consoled her. "There will be others, my sister."

"No, you promised me that one day I would become the Princess of Mehsia and now this," she said hurtfully. "Who is this Princess Celina?"

"She is the heir to the Isshi kingdom. She is the daughter of King Ramnah."

"What does she have that I don't have, my dear brother?" asked Lady Zorresia.

"Well, she is... she is not as talented as you are in the kitchen, my sister," said Lord Phillip cautiously searching for the right words to further avoid hurting his sister's feelings. "She could use a little meat on her bones and she has the most unusually large eyes."

Lady Zorresia laughed. "Oh brother, you do love me. I can tell by the way you are trying to protect my feelings. I can't imagine Prince Kishan would select someone so awkward." She smiled at her brother. "I do love Prince Kishan, but I guess I will have to settle for being a part of the wedding party, instead. Oh brother, I will volunteer to be the wedding planner. Do you think Prince Kishan and his new bride-to-be would agree?"

"Well, you must ask him or her for yourself. You are very creative and a good planner, too," replied Lord Phillip. He loved his sister and wanted to encourage her.

"I shall do so," replied Lady Zorresia. She hurried to the library and penned a letter to Princess Celina.

Lord Phillip smiled. His sister was strong willed just like their mother was, and despite her being brokenhearted, he knew that she would make Mehsia proud and serve as an excellent wedding planner. He reminisced about the day he promised his dying mother he would find his sister the perfect man to marry. Now, he thought his work was cut out for him because Prince Kishan was betrothed to another. He was disappointed that it was not his sister who would be walking down that aisle to marry the prince.

CHAPTER 10

"It's a lovely day for a picnic, indeed" said Princess Celina as she smiled at Prince Kishan.

"It is a lovely a day. I can see your beautiful eyes twinkling in the sunlight," replied Prince Kishan.

"Are you flirting with me, sir?" asked Princess Celina.

"Just a little frolic to stimulate the lady," said Prince Kishan. Irritated by the conversation between

Princess Celina and Prince Kishan, Lady Sari interrupted "Would you like a piece of fruit?

"Yes," replied Princess Celina.

"How about you, Prince Kishan, would you like a piece, too?" said Lady Sari.

"Yes, that would be nice," replied Prince Kishan.

Lady Sari gently handed Princess Celina a piece of fruit from the picnic basket. She grabbed an apple and tossed it toward Prince Kishan yelling, "Heads up!" She took off running outward into the meadows.

Prince Kishan barely caught the apple and said, "You little stinker." He then immediately began to chase after Lady Sari.

"Run, Sari, run fast!" yelled Princess Celina.

Lady Sari ran fast out into the meadows toward a hidden cave. "Bet you can't find me," she taunted the prince. Prince Kishan followed Lady Sari toward the cave. As he approached the cave, he yelled, "I will catch you, you little jokester."

Lady Sari remained silent and continued to hide in the cave until she saw a small animal. Frightened, she shouted, "Oh my lord," and ran into the arms of Prince Kishan, nearly knocking him down. She tightly hugged Prince Kishan. "Save me, my prince!" she cried.

"It's only a little mouse," said Prince Kishan as he picked it up by the tail and threw it outside the cave. Lady Sari continued to hold on to Prince Kishan. He swept her up into his arms and said "You are safe now, my lady."

Lady Sari looked Prince Kishan in the eyes with the sensual lust of a young virgin lady who has just been saved by her knight in shining armor. Lady Sari had always had a crush on Prince Kishan, but now she was in his arms and the feeling of love was in her eyes.

As Prince Kishan stared back into her eyes, he noticed she was not the innocent, playful little girl he had originally thought of her. "Instead," he thought, "Lady Sari is not a little girl at all." Prince Kishan noticed her big brown eyes and full lips, which triggered a strong sensual attraction towards the young lady. As he held her in his arms, Prince Kishan could feel the warmth of her body. He looked at her black curly hair and his eyes followed every curve of her face until he reached her perky breast and was drawn to the smell of innocence that flowed from her breath.

"Oh my God," said Prince Kishan as he swallowed deeply and blinked his eyes in disbelief. He suddenly realized that the feelings he was experiencing at this very moment were quite intense and different from those he felt for Princess Celina. He had never felt love before and wasn't sure if this feeling was it. But he did realize that he didn't feel the same toward Princess Celina nor any other lady, as matter of fact.

"What are you two doing?" asked Princess Celina as she entered the cave and saw Lady Sari in the arms of Prince Kishan.

"You can put me down now," said Lady Sari. "I saw a mouse and was frightened. The prince saved me!"

"Yes that is the story exactly," replied Prince Kishan awkwardly, shocked to see Prince Celina.

"Well now, I'm glad he accomplished that. Let us all return safely to our picnic area," said Princess Celina.

The trio left the cave and returned to the picnic area to continue eating their lunch. All during lunch,

Prince Kishan seemed distant and quiet.

"Cat got your tongue?" said Princess Celina.

"No," replied Prince Kishan.

"You seem to be in deep thought," said the princess.

"No, I'm just admiring the beauty of nature," said Prince Kishan as he looked over at Lady Sari. Lady Sari gazed back at him and then shamelessly looked at Princess Celina.

"Well, it's getting late. I think we must head back," said Princess Celina to break the silence. "I must start working on plans for the engagement feast. Oh, by the way, prince, I received a letter from a Lady Zorresia. She has offered to coordinate the engagement feast and be the wedding planner. Do you know of this Lady Zorresia?"

"Yes, she is quite close to my family. I think she would be an excellent wedding planner," replied Prince Kishan.

"Well, then it is done. I shall welcome her aboard," said Princess Celina.

The three gathered their things and rode their horses back to the palace. As they approached the front of the palace, the guardsmen unloaded their packs, while Prince Kishan assisted the two ladies as they dismounted their horses. First Prince Kishan offered Princess Celina his hand as she dismounted and headed toward the palace doors. While her back was turned, Prince Kishan excitedly grabbed Lady Sari around her waist more intimately and helped her dismount the horse.

Lady Sari closely held the prince around his neck as she slowly slid down with her legs wrapped around his long, lean body and landed on her feet. Lady Sari looked him in the eyes with hope of love. Prince Kishan followed the two ladies toward the front door. Princess Celina told Lady Sari to go inside the palace and that she would be in shortly to read with her in the library.

"Goodbye Prince," said Lady Sari in a weepy, soft voice.

Prince Kishan softly replied, "Goodbye to you, too."

Prince Kishan and Lady Sari struggled with their goodbyes. Both of them were toiling with heavy hearts full of emotions. Princess Celina closed the door and turned to Prince Kishan to thank him for a wonderful picnic. But Prince Kishan could only hear the voice of Lady Sari and could only see the emotions in her eyes. Princess Kishan stood on the doorstep staring at Princess

Celina as she confessed her love for him. He stared obliviously as her lips moved, but he didn't hear one word she said. He could only focus on his feelings for Lady Sari.

"Good bye, prince," said Princess Celina.

"Good bye, princess", replied Prince Kishan as he mounted his horse to travel back to Mehsia.

CHAPTER 11

"Welcome ladies," said Patel.

"Hello Patel," replied the three young ladies in unison

"Welcome, my queen." Patel bowed in respect to Queen Mayora. "Please have a seat." She pointed towards the sitting area. "I will gather some fabric swatches—hopefully they will be to the bride's liking." Patel smiled at Princess Celina.

"Yes, bring the most beautiful ones with lots of patterns and lace," said Princess Celina.

"Bring the most expensive, quality fabrics," called Queen Mayora. "Your father has ordered me to buy the best for his little girl," she said to Celina.

"Oh, thank you, Mother," said Princess Celina.

"Oh, thank you, Mother," repeated Countess Tierra and Lady Sari as they giggled and snickered between themselves.

Patel returned with rolls of colored silk and lacey patterned fabric.

"These are beautiful. Look, Mother, how do you like this one?" asked the princess as she handed the roll of fabric to Queen Mayora.

"Is this your choice for the wedding dress?" asked Queen Mayora.

"Patel, there is someone knocking at the door," said Countess Tierra.

"Who might that be? I have no customers scheduled today. Please forgive me, my queen. I tried to protect your privacy," said Patel.

"It is probably the wedding planner I invited," said Princess Celina.

"Wedding planner? We have not discussed this," said Queen Mayora, surprised.

"She was recommended by Prince Kishan and his family."

"That seems very untraditional," said Queen Mayora. "It is always the bride and her family's responsibility to plan the wedding!"

"I will plan my wedding, Mother. She will only be assisting me," said the princess calmly.

"I don't like this one bit. I don't think we should have a wedding planner," said the queen.

"Hello everyone," said Lady Zorresia, as she entered the room. Everyone turned and looked at her from head to toe and twice over. Lady Zorresia was dressed in a bright pink garment with yellow chrysanthemums in the pattern of her cloak. She had the biggest and brightest smile on her round, full face.

"Um, hello. You must be Lady Zorresia, the wedding planner," said Patel.

"Yes, indeed, my lady. I am," said Lady Zorresia excitedly.

"Please join us," said Patel.

"Oh thank you," replied Lady Zorresia. "How beautiful are all the fabrics!" she said as she carefully critiqued each swatch.

"Thank you," said Patel. "I made each one myself." She snatched the fabric out of Lady Zorresia's hands.

Ignoring the rude gesture of Patel, Lady Zorresia said, "Well princess, shall we get started?" "What are your wedding colors?"

"I like fuchsia and I have chosen chrysanthemum as my flower," replied Princess Celina excitedly.

"Just as I am wearing," said Lady Zorresia. "We have a lot in common—both in clothing and men."

Puzzled by Lady Zorresia's comments, Princess Celina asked, "How long have you known Prince Kishan, my lady?"

"Well, I've known him most of my life. We grew up together," replied Lady Zorresia. She daydreamed and escaped the moment by telling her childhood stories about Prince Kishan. "I remember the very first day that we met." Lady Zorresia told her story with joy and excitement, but most importantly, the story was full of love. "I was running to catch a butterfly, when I fell on my knee. There were two little boys who just pointed at me and laughed. But Prince Kishan, he came over and offered his hand to pick me up. He dusted off my knee and asked if I was okay. I was just a little peasant girl, but he was royalty—my little prince. I looked up into his eyes and said, 'I'm okay, thank you.'" The ladies sat in silence as Lady Zorresia told her simple, but caring and compassionate story about the prince. Anyone could see the love and passion in her eyes.

Everyone was intrigued except Countess Tierra. Suddenly, she interrupted. "It seems the lady has a fancy for the prince."

Embarrassed by the countess's remarks, Lady Zorresia quickly said, "Oh nonsense, my lady. He is like a brother to me. My family has always served his family in the royal court."

"Well," sighed Princess Celina in relief. "That was a lovely story. Please do excuse my younger sister for being terribly rude. Let's get back to the wedding planning, shall we?"

"Would anyone like a cup of my special tea?" asked Patel.

"That would be wonderful," replied Queen Mayora.

"Do you know the prince?" Lady Zorresia asked Countess Tierra.

"Why, of course I have met him—he's marrying my sister, as you know," replied the countess sharply.

"What type of name is Zorresia, anyway?

"Zorresia was my grandmother's name. It means 'poisoned one,'" said Lady Zorresia creepily.

"How strange," said Countess Tierra.

"Well, if you like, you can call me Lady Z," said Lady Zorresia.

"Lady Z, I like it," said the countess, nodding and smiling in agreement.

Patel returned to the room with the tea. "I know the royal family, as well. As a matter of fact—his mother, Queen Jacuma, purchases her fabric from my shop. He was just here the other day to pick up her order while the countess was visiting me."

"The prince was here?" asked both Princess Celina and Lady Sari, surprised.

Queen Mayora, looking over at Lady Sari,

observed a sparkle in her youngest daughter's eyes as she spoke of the prince. "What could that sparkle in her eye possibly mean?" thought the queen. "Maybe she is infatuated with the prince. How cute and innocent. Oh well, he is awfully handsome."

Meanwhile, Princess Celina turned to Countess Tierra. "You never mentioned to me that you spoke with the prince."

"Why yes," said Patel, smiling. "And we had a wonderful, friendly conversation."

Princess Celina approached the countess and tersely asked, "What did you tell him about me?"

"Nothing," replied Countess Tierra as she turned away.

"You liar. What did you tell him?" shouted Princess Celina angrily as she grabbed Tierra by the shoulders and turned her sister toward her. Countess Tierra did not reply. Princess Celina slapped her on the face.

Shocked by her sister's actions, Tierra began to cry and shouted, "You are just like Father. I told you, I said nothing—Mother, please stop her!"

Queen Mayora commanded Princess Celina to stop hurting her sister and control her temper.

Countess Tierra ran over to her mother, shouting at Princess Celina, "You are beautiful on the outside, but ugly on the inside. You are your father's child and I hate you for it."

"You are jealous of me," replied Princess Celina, "and you will do whatever to destroy my relationship with the prince."

"He is my friend," replied Countess Tierra.

"Princess, please contain yourself. Your sister stated she only befriended the prince, nothing more," said Queen Mayora as she consoled Countess Tierra.

The queen took pride in defending Countess Tierra. Of course she was her 'favorite daughter' but she could not resist the opportunity to get revenge against King Ramnah by chastising his 'favorite daughter'— Princess Celina.

Lady Sari noticed that the queen feverishly protected Countess Tierra in way she had never seen before. She felt a sense of loneliness and abandonment. She'd always known Princess Celina was her father's favorite girl, but Sari thought *she* was her mother's favorite. But after observing her mother's emotional outburst and defensive behaviors, she now knew that her mother's favorite was Tierra, not her.

"I think we should have our tea now," Lady Sari said sadly.

"That would be most appropriate." Patel poured the tea and served the ladies pastries.

Hurt and disappointed, Lady Sari sat quietly sipping her tea. "Princess Celina is my father's favorite girl, and Countess Tierra is my mother's favorite girl," she thought to herself. "And I? I belong to no one. What a shameful pity."

She sat quietly remembering her 13th birthday celebration. Her mother had the servants to baked her a cake. King Ramnah had the craftsmen built her very own pink carriage with her name embossed on each side door. It had large wheels trimmed with gold, and 36 inch spinners, with plush velvet interior seat cushions. The smoothest ride in all the lands. Built with love, especially for daddy's little girl. At least that is what she thought at the time.

But naively, the young lady did not know the impact of the unforgettable impression she had left on the mind of the handsome young prince and the trials and tribulations that awaited her in the very near future.

CHAPTER 12

The journey from Isshi to Mehsia had become familiar to the prince. He had travelled it numerous times over the last several months during his courtship with the princess. But this time, the journey was different. It was full of timeless thoughts. The tapestry of the forest was vibrant, and the colors of the sky and the trees were vivid. The trees seemed greener this time. The leaves were happily dancing in tune with the mild wind and seemed to be humming a melody of love.

"Heavenly hearts have joined as one, you have fell in love with the little lovely one."

These thoughts and his experiences with Lady Sari lingered in the forefront of his mind. "Why won't the images of her just go away? It is Princess Celina I am betrothed to," he thought as he struggled with his conflicting feelings. He began to sing out loudly in the forest, trying to interrupt the constant visions of Sari's beautiful eyes. All the way home, Prince Kishan kept imagining the time he had spent with Lady Sari in the cave—how intrigued he was by her.

As the journey slowly came to a close, so did his love for Princess Celina. Prince Kishan began to question his feelings for the princess and more and more affirmed his love for Lady Sari. He argued with himself and debated why he had gone on that picnic anyway. He concluded that, if he had not gone on the stupid picnic, then he would not have even been in this situation in the first place. By the time Prince Kishan had arrived at home in Mehsia, he was surely convinced that he was in love with Lady Sari and not in love with Princess Celina. He thought, "What am I going to do about this problem?"

As Prince Kishan arrived home, he decided he would talk these problems over with his father. He thought maybe it was time for a "man-to-man" conversation.

"Hello my son," said King Hubaka.

"Hello Father," replied the prince as he approached his father who was sitting in the parlor reading a book. The two men greeted each other with love and respect.

"How was your picnic with Princess Celina?" asked King Hubaka.

"Oh just perfect, Father," replied the prince solemnly.

"You know Princess Celina is quite beautiful," said the king.

"But Father, you are the one who told me never to measure a woman by her outer beauty," replied the prince.

The king laughed. "I guess you do listen to this old man."

"Father, may I ask you a question?"

"Of course, my son," replied the king.

"Never mind, Father," said the prince as he walked around the parlor in deep thought.

King Hubaka sensed something was wrong, but didn't press the issue. He thought that the prince would ask his questions when the time was right.

The prince then turned and asked, "Where is Mother?

"She is in her chambers," said King Hubaka.

Prince Kishan quickly left his father's side and headed straightway to his mother's chambers.

"Hello Mother," said the prince.

"Hello handsome," said the queen joyfully. "And what is the reason for you blessing me with your presence today?"

"I have something I need to discuss with you. I don't know how to say this, but—"said the prince.

"Before you begin," the queen interrupted, "have you considered your dowry?"

"My dowry?" said the prince.

"Yes silly, the offering for the princess's hand in marriage," replied the queen. "You must offer your most prized possession."

"I have offered my most prized possessions. The princess will have my heart forever. What more can a man offer?"

"No, my son, I am referring to your valuable treasures," laughed the queen. "You must ask your father for the Medallion and offer it as the dowry."

"Mother, that is totally insane," replied the prince calmly. "Surely no one ever expects to receive such a valuable item for their daughter's hand in marriage—not even the infamous King Ramnah. It is the most valuable treasure of the Mehsia kingdom and is not for sale," said scornfully. "I know, I will offer my two prize horses."

"Oh how silly," said the queen. "Princess Celina is charming and lovely, my son. You have chosen the greatest treasure of the infamous King Ramnah; surely she is worth more. I can't believe you will be married in a few weeks. Can you believe it, my little boy will be a husband." The queen placed her hand on the prince's face.

"Mother, stop it, just stop it. I must tell you that I don't want to marry Princess Celina!" he shouted. "I don't love her," he said lowering his voice, hoping to gain sympathy from his overzealous mother.

But the queen's response was just the opposite. The queen was outraged. She slapped his face and shouted, "Now you hear me. It is time for you to grow up and realize that life is not all fun and frolic!" she yelled. "I need you to marry that damn princess."

"You need me to marry her?" repeated the prince. "Why Mother? Is there something you are not sharing with me?"

"Listen to me, son, your father and I are in danger," said the queen softly so that the servants could not hear their conversation.

"What do you mean, Mother?" asked the prince.

"We have lost the war and King Ramnah has decided to spare your father's and my lives only if you marry his daughter, Princess Celina," cried the queen.

"Are you serious, Mother? Is my proposed marriage to Princess Celina, some type of barter with King Ramnah? Have you resorted to trading me like property?" asked Prince Kishan as tears filled his eyes with the hurt and pain of betrayal. He adored his mother and was now disappointed in her. "Does Father know about these threats from King Ramnah?"

"No, my son, I didn't want to bother your father with this," replied Queen Jacuma. "Your father is too old and frail to fight back, and our armies have already been defeated. We can't beat King Ramnah's armies!"

"I will not stand by and let that King Ramnah destroy our kingdom. As heir to the throne of Mehsia, I will take these matters into my own hands," said Prince Kishan.

"No!" cried the queen. "He will destroy you. You are my only son and I can't afford to lose you! Our only hope is for you to marry, Prince Celina. That will solve this problem."

"Mother, please do not force this marriage upon your only son. I don't love her!" shouted Prince Kishan. "I will go to King Ramnah and defend our family name." He walked over to the desk, opened the drawer, took a gold dagger out of a box, and shoved it into his belt.

"Please son, oh please no. King Ramnah is a dangerous person!" cried the queen desperately as she grabbed Prince Kishan by his cloak. "He will surely kill you!"

"No Mother, this is my battle," replied Prince Kishan with courage and stamina.

"Just marry her, please," pleaded Queen Jacuma as she fell to floor in desperation.

But Prince Kishan did not respond to his mother's attempts to stopping him. He loosened her hands from his cloak and slammed the door as he left the palace.

CHAPTER 13

Raging with anger, Prince Kishan rode fearlessly through the forest and meadows to return to the Isshi Palace. This time his journey was not so pleasant. He was filled with fire and passion for war and the forest felt his wrath. The wind blew forcefully. The trees were standing tall like soldiers in an army, and the leaves were chanting courageous thoughts to build up his warrior strength.

"Fight young prince, fight them all; Fight young prince, you will not fall," the forest trees chanted.

Unable to contain himself, the prince yelled back to them, "I will slay the king and kill them all, I will not let my kingdom fall!"

His voice rang out for miles, echoing in the air, frightening the animals in the forest while simultaneously awakening the ferocious beast that dwelled inside him.

Arriving late in the evening at the palace gate, Prince Kishan was met by the palace guard. The prince said to the guard, "I must see King Ramnah immediately."

"The king is with his court," replied the guard harshly.

"I must see the king now. It is important!" yelled Prince Kishan.

The guard could see the anger flowering in the prince's eyes. "Aren't you the prince who is betrothed to marry Princess Celina?" he asked.

"Yes, sir, and I must see the king," replied Prince Kishan.

"Okay, I guess it won't hurt anything. I will summon the king," said the guard. He soon returned. "The king will see you in the parlor."

Prince Kishan aggressively pushed his way through the palace doors, shoving the guard. He entered the parlor, but King Ramnah was not there. Prince Kishan waited impatiently and, just as he decided to exit the parlor and search for King Ramnah in the palace, the king entered.

"Hello Prince Kishan. What brings you here so late? I know you can't wait to marry my daughter, but to call upon her at this hour is a little eager, even for a young sought-after prince like you."

"I have not come to see the princess," replied Prince Kishan bitterly. "It is you I have come to see. I have come to defend my family's honor." He drew his dagger from his belt and pointed it at King Ramnah.

King Ramnah was shocked by Prince Kishan actions. "Son, careful with that weapon. You don't want to do this. I am the king here," said King Ramnah in a soft, low voice, cautious not to anger the prince. "You won't get past the palace door before my guards kill you. Therefore, please put the weapon away."

Prince Kishan tightly gripped the handle of the dagger and pressed its sharp tip into the king's neck. "You threatened my mother and my father with murder. And now, I shall kill you."

"Young man, you don't understand," exclaimed King Ramnah cautiously.

"No King, I do understand. Your behaviors have angered the very warrior of my soul and I will do anything to protect my family," replied Prince Kishan.

"Did you speak with your mother?" King Ramnah asked as he slowly raised his cup and splashed his drink into Prince Kishan's eyes.

Prince Kishan lowered his dagger and covered his eyes because they burned with pain from the wine. King Ramnah hit the prince across the face with the cup, and blood began to flow down the side of the prince's face.

King Ramnah took the dagger and placed it against the prince's neck. Grinding his teeth together and holding the prince from behind, he said in a stern voice, "You listen carefully, young prince. I will say this only once. If you ever raise your dagger to me again, I will rip your head off and send it to your beloved mother in a box."

Prince Kishan struggled to loosen himself from the strong, tight hold King Ramnah had around his neck, but was unsuccessful. King Ramnah jerked Prince Kishan and pressed the dagger deeper into his neck, pricking his skin. Prince Kishan felt a piercing pain in his neck but could not move.

"You will sit and listen to me, boy," King Ramnah continued. Prince Kishan did not respond. "Do—you—hear me?" said the king angrily as he pushed the dagger deeper into the prince's neck.

"Yes, sir," replied Prince Kishan bitterly.

"Do I have your word?" King Ramnah asked, tightening his forearm around the prince's neck, this time cutting off his breathing.

"Yes!" gasped the prince.

King Ramnah released the pressure of his forearm and lowered the dagger.

144

Prince Kishan gave a sigh of relief as he held his neck from the pain. King Ramnah threw him a cloth to ripe the blood from his face, then walked over to the vase to pour them each a cup of wine. King Ramnah then turned and walked over to Prince Kishan, politely handing him the cup. "Here, drink. It might help soothe your wounds.

Prince Kishan took the cup and thirstily guzzled down the wine. "More please," he said.

King Ramnah poured another cup of wine and gave it to the prince. Then, exhausted, he sat down in the chair opposite Prince Kishan.

"I am not your enemy," he said. "Your enemies are friendly to your kingdom and dwell there. Someday you will be king with great power. Then, and only then, will you begin to know the hearts of men and experience the sensual trap of a seductive woman. It is during these times when you have power that you will be betrayed by those who are closest to you. And that, my young prince, is the worst curse to any king," he said sympathetically.

"Did you threaten to kill my parents if I don't marry Prince Celina?" Prince Kishan asked the weary king.

King Ramnah laughed. "Prince, have you not heard the words I have said to you? I have agreed to an arrangement with those close to you in your very own kingdom. And with that, my friend, I wouldn't necessarily consider it a threat."

Prince Kishan interrogated the king. "What are the terms of this arrangement? Who made these arrangements? Who has the gall to make arrangements on behalf of the Kingdom of Mehsia without my father's permission? Who, I ask?"

"The terms of this arrangement are complex," replied King Ramnah. "You see, my young lad, the terms of the arrangement are dependent upon your willingness to marry my daughter, Princess Celina."

"So, you did threaten to kill my parents if I do not marry your precious Prince Celina," asked the prince, astonished, as he stood up to confront King Ramnah.

"Please, please—sit down," demanded King Ramnah. "There are much bigger issues here to consider. The threat of death upon your parents and your obligations to marry the princess are only means to an end. There are greater treasures at stake here. Don't worry—your parents will be okay if the terms of the agreement are met. I think I have said enough."

The king stood up and escorted Prince Kishan to the door. "Remember, young prince, it might prove very costly to your kingdom if you don't marry my daughter. The terms of my agreement with your kingdom were brought to me by those closest to you. Speak with Ouray—maybe he will clarify your obligations to me."

As Prince Kishan proceeded to leave the palace, he suddenly stopped, slowly turned, and asked the king curiously, "If I ask your daughter for her hand in marriage, what might you accept as the dowry?"

King Ramnah looked deeply into the eyes of the naive prince and cryptically replied, "That which is most valuable to your kingdom."

Puzzled by the King's words, Prince Kishan exited the palace and headed straightway to visit Ouray.

King Ramnah returned to his chair to reflect on the conversation with the prince. Shortly afterward, he was interrupted by a visit from Princess Celina.

"Father, who were you speaking with?" she asked as she entered the parlor.

"Just handling a few problems with the men," replied the king.

"Oh Father, you are a dedicated king," said Prince Celina as she hugged then gently kissed her father on the cheek. She then gracefully kneeled down in front of him and rested her head in his lap. "I do love you, Father."

"I love you too, my princess," replied the king.

"Father, may I speak with you regarding love?" asked Princess Celina.

"Yes, my love, what bothers your pretty little head," replied the King, stroking her hair.

"Love is so complex," stated the princess. "Father, please tell of how your heart felt when you fell in love."

King Ramnah hesitated because, unbeknownst to his daughter, who sat in anticipation of hearing her father's love story, the story of the king's first love wouldn't include his wife, Queen Mayora. So instead of immediately replying to his daughter, King Ramnah laid his head back on the chair to relax and begin to reminisce of the day he'd met his first love—Queen Jacuma. Adding nothing to the statements made by the princess and surely not answering her questions, the king could only say, "Yes, love is complex."

Surprised by her father's limited response to her question, the princess raised her head and looked up at her father. "Please Father, tell me more. How did you know for sure that you were in love with Mother?"

Continuing to relax with his head back, the king replied, "Things were very different in my early days. Things were so difficult for a young prince like me. Soooo complex," he softly whispered. King Ramnah intentionally didn't answer Princess Celina's questions. Instead, he merely closed his eyes and fell into a deep slumber.

CHAPTER 14

Meanwhile, Prince Kishan had arrived at Chateau Hanpeul, the dark and hauntingly creepy house of Ouray, the sorcerer. Chateau Hanpeul was once owned by foreigners from far away who had fled their native country and settled in Mehsia. The native people were extremely shy and preferred to roam around in the darkness of the night. They were small in stature with very large brain powers and keen sensorial intelligence. Many of the unisexual Hanpeulians mysteriously mated with the eunuchs and had borne offspring with the most unusual features. But despite their extreme features, they were the most intelligent creatures in all the Mehsia lands. Some said that they were the force behind many of Ouray's mystical endeavors.

As Prince Kishan approached the uncanny chateau, he could hear loud voices, laughter, and feasting coming from within. He dismounted his horse and ferociously kicked opened the front door. Everyone inside the chateau was shocked. They immediately stopped what they were doing and turned their undivided attention to Prince Kishan who stood authoritatively in the doorway.

Breaking the silence and the stares, Ouray said, "Well, well, we have company. The bumbling idiot has finally arrived." Ouray lay nestled between three female creatures as they played sensually with each other. Everyone in the room began to laugh hysterically at his comments.

"I'm glad you find my presence amusing. But you will soon discover that my presence is important and lacks the need for humor," replied the prince. "I must speak with you immediately."

"Then speak," said Ouray.

"In private," demanded the prince.

"We're among friends. Speak, prince. Please do tell us what's on your mind, huh?" said Ouray sarcastically.

"I just returned from Isshi, where I spoke with King Ramnah regarding an agreement you made on behalf of the Mehsia Kingdom," said the prince.

Surprised, Ouray suddenly pushed away the creatures surrounding him and stood on his feet. "I think we need to speak in private, follow me."

Prince Kishan followed Ouray into a dark room in the back of the Chateau. Ouray lit a candle and offered Prince Kishan a seat.

"No offense, but I would prefer to stand," said Prince Kishan. "I demand that you divulge to me the terms of the deal you made with King Ramnah."

Ouray calmly walked around the room with his hand under his chin, deep in thought. "I guess there is no easy way to say this." He then suddenly turned to the prince as said in a deep, demonic powerful fiery voice, "You and your kingdom will finally be destroyed." Ouray's physical characteristics had also drastically changed. He flesh was scaly, his eyes were piercing

155

black, and his facial features portrayed characteristics of a demon.

Shocked by Ouray's sudden transformation, Prince Kishan immediately drew his sword and assumed the warrior's battle position.

Ouray continued in his demonic voice, "I have traded the most valuable item that Mehsia kingdom owns—the Medallion." He laughed. "If you don't marry Princess Celina and deliver the Medallion to King Ramnah as the dowry, he will kill Queen Jacuma and your worthless father, King Hubaka."

Stunned by Ouray's words, Prince Kishan replied, "You traitor, I shall take your head off!" He swung his sword at Ouray.

Ouray roared with anger and swiftly ascended into the air while completely transforming into a demonic dragon-like creature. "You are pathetic. Do you think a mere sword is a match for my powers?" he roared. He lifted Prince Kishan off the ground and forcefully slammed his body against the wall using his invisible powers. Ouray used his dragon tail and wrapped it around Prince Kishan's neck, choking him while lifting him up in air and bringing him closer until they were face to face. Looking into the prince's eyes, Ouray exclaimed hatefully, "I will destroy the Mehsia kingdom and your father for ruining my life!"

Struggling to breathe and straining to speak, Prince Kishan asked, "What have my parents done to you to deserve such betrayal?"

"Many years ago," said Ouray, "your father— because of his weakness as a king—allowed people to run rampant without order or law in the kingdom.

Indecent men were killing and performing unnatural sex acts with eunuchs and forcing other men to do the same. My father, who was a holy man full of life, was forced by these men to rape a young hanpuel. He begged them not to allow such things to happen, but they tied her down and brutally beat him until he committed these heinous acts upon the young hanpuel. The young hanpuel eventually gave birth to an infant that was half man, half beast!" Ouray roared. "Is the picture clearer to you yet, My Prince?"Ouray violently threw Prince Kishan onto the floor.

Prince Kishan moaned with pain from the thrust to the ground. He was wounded, but he stood up aggressively and again positioned himself in the warrior battle stance.

"This is not your fight, Prince Kishan," yelled Ouray. "My fight is with your father!"

"My father is frail and cannot fight for himself. I will defend the Kingdom of Mehsia and protect the Medallion," said Prince Kishan defensively.

Ouray laughed. "Young prince, young fool. You are no match for my powers or my intelligence. The Mehsia kingdom will be destroyed!"

It had now become apparent to Prince Kishan that he and Princess Celina were pawns in a plot by Ouray and King Ramnah to take control of and destroy the Kingdom of Mehsia. He realized that the future of his kingdom and his family's life depended upon him marrying Princess Celina and presenting the Mehsia Medallion to King Ramnah as the dowry for the princess's hand in marriage. He thought what an awfully high price it was to pay for marriage to someone he didn't love.

Prince Kishan stumbled outside the chateau, mounted his horse, and rode fiercely back to Isshi to see Princess Celina. Maybe, just maybe, he thought, he would be able to convince her to call off the wedding.

CHAPTER 15

As Princess Celina lay resting in her bed, she heard a tap on the window.

"My lady, my lady," whispered the prince.

Princess Celina got out bed and went over to the window. There, she noticed Prince Kishan climbing up the garden ladder to her bedroom window. With excitement in her eyes, she opened the window and whispered, 'My love, please be careful." She helped Prince Kishan through the window and into her bedroom.

"My darling, what brings to my chambers this late in the evening?" asked the princess.

The prince quietly replied, "I must speak with you. It is very important." He took her by the hand and led her over to the bed. "Please sit," he said as he kneeled before her. "Princess Celina, do you love me?" he asked.

"Why of course I do, silly," replied the princess.

"How could you possibly love me?" said the prince hastily. "You barely know who I am. Why do you love me?"

"Well, because—I love you because," said the princess as she looked away confused.

"Please look me in the eyes and tell me why you want to spend the rest of your life with me," said the prince forcefully as he firmly clasped her wrist. "Tell me that when you look into my eyes you see my soul and our hearts beat as one. Tell me!" he demanded.

"You are hurting me, Kishan!" cried the princess as she resisted his firm hold. "I don't have to answer these types of questions—you should know why I want to be married. Marriage is a ritual in our kingdom. For years every princess in our family has been married when they reached my age without ever knowing the meaning of true love," she said softly.

"They married without love in their hearts and out of blind rituals?" asked the Prince, surprised.

"Father says love and marriage are complex," replied Princess Celina.

"I don't want to hear any logic your father might use to justify his self-serving actions," said Prince Kishan angrily as he stood up and turned his back to the princess."I don't understand why you are so bitter at my father—and why all of these questions?" said the princess. "Don't you want to marry me, Prince Kishan?"

The prince did not reply. He merely turned toward her and pleaded, "Princess, you must call off the wedding."

Surprised and hurt by his words, Princess Celina began to cry hysterically. "No! No! I will not do such a thing. How will the people look at this? I will be made a mockery! Are you in love with someone else?" she wept. "Please Prince Kishan, please—don't you love me?" Princess Celina began to disrobe, taking off her nightgown in a desperate pled to seduce the prince.

As she stood naked before him, the prince encapsulated the beauty of her body with his eyes. He was spellbound by her nakedness. He had had never seen a woman's naked body before, although many thought he had. He was still a virgin and so was the princess. Prince Kishan briefly beheld her curvaceous hips and her full breast. "Celina, do you have no dignity?" he said. "Please cover yourself." He quickly turned away and covered his eyes.

Princess Celina was devastated by the prince's rejection. Never had she thought that the young prince would reject her sensual advances. She shamefully put on her nightgown and fell onto the bed, crying uncontrollably.

Disappointed in the princess's obsession of wanting to be married for tradition and for ritual, the prince went over to her bedside and quietly offered kind words. "Princess, I must leave now, but please trust me. I never, ever meant to hurt you." Prince Kishan was hoping that his apology would provide some level of comfort to the sobbing and heart-broken princess.

But unfortunately, the words pierced her heart even deeper and the young princess wailed even louder, startling the prince. Prince Kishan tried to console her, but he could not bear to see the hurt he had caused her, so he quietly left through the window.

It was late in the night and that was the time Countess Tierra did most of her studying and reading. She was an avid reader of all types of ancient books and scrolls, and symbolic love stories were her favorite. As she sat reading, Countess Tierra could hear noises coming from Princess Celina's chambers. She put on her robe and quietly walked down to her sister's chambers.

"Princess, Princess?" she barely whispered. "Are you okay?" Hearing no reply, the countess entered Princess Celina's chamber and noticed that she was crying.

"Why are you weeping? Princess?" asked Countess Tierra softly as she sat down on the bed next to her sister.

The princess immediately embraced Countess Tierra. "It's the prince. He has asked me to call off the wedding."

"Why?" Countess Tierra asked, surprised.

"I don't know—he said something about true love," babbled Princess Celina, trying to explain as the tears flowed from her eyes. "I am so confused. I thought he loved me."

"Oh Celina, he does love you. Maybe he is just getting cold feet," said Countess Tierra.

"Oh yes, maybe that's it," said the princess, immediately perking up. She hugged her sister excitedly. "Mother always said you were the smart one, and this holds true. Thank you for making me see the other side of my prince's heart. Thank you, I love you so much."

"I love you, too," said Countess Tierra. "Rest now and don't worry yourself with these things. You are only days from being the PRINCESS OF MEHSIA!" she exclaimed loudly. The two ladies smiled and Countess Tierra tucked the princess back into the bed and blew out the lantern.

As Countess Tierra walked back to her chambers, she felt puzzled by the prince's request to call off the wedding. She knew this spelled trouble in the lovers' paradise but didn't want to further upset her sister. As she lay in bed, she couldn't help but wonder, "Why?" She thought maybe the prince realized that being married would be overwhelming for him as a young man; or maybe his parents didn't approve of the princess; or maybe he was really in love with someone else. These types of questions continued to plague her mind.

"Hmmm, who might the prince be in love with besides the princess? Maybe it is Lady Zorresia? Or maybe it is a lady in his royal court? Or could it possibly be me?"

The countess smiled to herself and began to fantasize about how it would feel to kiss the prince. She envisioned them kissing in her mind like a romantic fairytale. She imagined how she would fall into his arms and softly press her lips against his lips. The moment would be perfect, enrapturing them both into a mystical realm of love. He would adore and desire only her—and not for her beauty, but for her intelligence. He would long to spend every waking moment of his life with her, only her. She dreamed of how she would use her intellect to read poetry to him and help him develop and decode complex war strategies. Countess Tierra continued to bask in the hopeful journey of a love affair with Prince Kishan until she fell asleep.

CHAPTER 16

As Prince Kishan rode through the meadows back to Mehsia, he noticed he was being followed by someone riding a grey stallion and dressed in a black hooded cloak. Unaware who this person was, the prince began to ride faster to place distance between the unknown person and himself. As the person gained ground and came closer, the prince rode faster.

"Sir, sir," the voice cried out. "Please slow down. I must speak with you."

"Who are you?" asked Prince Kishan.

"I am surprised you do not recognize my voice," the mystery person replied.

Prince Kishan smiled. He recognized the sweet sounding voice of a lady. "Follow me into the cave," he said.

As the lady dismounted her horse and entered the cave, Prince Kishan grabbed her from behind and pulled her close to kiss her. But the woman struggled and shouted, "Take your hands off me, you pervert!"

Surprised by the woman's reaction, Prince Kishan pulled back the hood to reveal the mystery lady. "Queen!" he shouted. "Please pardon my behavior."

"Who did you think I was? One of your lovers?" asked the queen tersely as she straightened out her clothing.

"Uh, no, My Queen," replied the prince embarrassed. "I thought you were, of course, Princess Celina. Please, I beg that you forgive my behavior. What brings you into the forest at this late hour? And why on earth were you following me?"

"My young prince, there are many secrets that stir the angry spirits of my soul. But where should one start?" said the queen as she struggled to find a beginning point for her secret story. "I guess there is only one place to start and that would be at the beginning." The queen sighed in relief and sat down on top of a large rock in the cave. "You mustn't marry my daughter, Princess Celina," she said regretfully.

The prince was completely taken aback by the queen's words and almost lost his balance, so he slumped down on top of a rock and braced himself. He thought maybe the queen had overheard his earlier conversations with Princess Celina. Or maybe the queen knew of his true love? Puzzled, he thought maybe this would be a good time to confess everything about the secret agreement between the two kingdoms.

"Yes, there are many secrets that exist between our kingdoms, and—"Just as the prince was about to confess the terms of the secret deal between Isshi and Mehsia, the queen abruptly interrupted him and began to tell the true secret story that had plagued the two kingdoms for years and the main reason for the war.

"Years ago," she began, "there was a young maiden whom King Ramnah was very much in love with. But her family was not of royalty, thereby making her unacceptable to marry the young king. Despite every forbidden word and warning from the young king's parents to leave this young maiden alone, the king continued to see her. They would sneak away together and spend time in the meadows for hours at a time. No one noticed this innocent and playful love affair until the young maiden became pregnant with child. Then all hell broke loose. Once Queen Lana, King Ramnah's mother, God bless her soul, got word of this young maiden's pregnancy, she became furious and demanded that the young maiden, her unborn child, and her family be banned from the Kingdom of Isshi. Queen Lana also demanded that the guardsmen kill the child upon its birth. Shortly thereafter, King Ramnah and I were married. I was so happy!"

She began to cry. "I was living in a fairytale that would soon turn into a nightmare. Months went by and when the guardsmen got word that the baby had been

175

born, they headed out to the house to kill the child as they'd been ordered by Queen Lana. But King Putal, King Ramnah's father told the men to bring the child to him upon its birth. King Putal basically forced that child into my perfect fairytale," said Queen Mayora bitterly. "And from that day on, that child became my worst nightmare. This bastard child innocently captured my husband's heart and immediately became the center of his life. He utterly loves and adores her to this very day," said the queen with tears in her eyes. She sat on top of the rock in silence, looking pathetically at Prince Kishan.

The prince then softly asked as his voice nervously trembled, "What happened to the child's mother?"

"Well, the young maiden was told that the baby died at birth, and she went on to live her life far away from the kingdom of Isshi."

Now, tears begin to slowly roll down his face. He was hurt and his heart was heavy with anguish. He slid off the rock and onto the ground, covering his face to shield his tears. With the help of Queen Mayora, he had pieced the puzzle together and he didn't like the picture.

Queen Mayora continued her story. "Years after your mother married your father, she later discovered that her baby had not died. But by that time it was too late, and King Ramnah had forbid her to see Princess Celina. He told her that, if she ever told Princess Celina the truth, he would kill her, kill your father, and destroy the Kingdom of Mehsia. To this day, King Hubaka, your father, and many others do not know that Queen Jacuma's bastard daughter is Princess Celina."

Feelings of betrayal overwhelmed Prince Kishan. He could not hold back his feelings any longer. He felt hopeless. He had been betrayed by his mother—Queen Jacuma. He struggled with how to cope with his feelings. He couldn't possibly behead his own mother or draw his dagger against her. This was new territory for Prince Kishan and it was difficult for him to deal with. But he did remember the words of King Ramnah, which rang loudly in his mind: *"It is during these times when you have power that you will be betrayed by those who are closest to you. And that, my young prince, is the worst curse for any king."*

Distraught, the prince dropped his head into his hands and cried like a young boy. "How could my own mother deceive me and my father?" he thought.

Queen Mayora continued, "I have lived with these lies for years. Every time I set eyes upon her, I'm reminded of my husband's true love, which is sadly not me as his wife," cried the queen as she wiped her tears.

The two heard a sound outside the cave. Prince Kishan immediately jumped up and ran outside to see who was there. "Who's there?" he called out. "Is anyone there?" But no one answered.

Frightened that someone might have overheard her conversation with the prince, the queen whispered, "It is getting late and I must get back to the palace. The king will be sending guardsmen to search for me shortly."

Prince Kishan helped Queen Mayora onto her horse.

The queen then smiled. "Maybe Countess Tierra would make you a better wife."

"Maybe," replied the prince sadly. "Maybe, My Queen," he softly repeated as Queen Mayora rode off on her horse.

Confused, the Prince regained his composure wiped his eyes and began his journey back to Mehisa. All the while, he wondered what he was going to say to the Princess at the feast. "Should he call off the event?", he thought.

CHAPTER 17

Hundreds of people gathered outside the Cristo M' Delio Chateau to get a glimpse of the young princess betrothed to the handsome, sought after Prince Kishan. Most of the people in the Kingdom of Mehsia had never seen the princess and waited anxiously outside the grand chateau to catch a glimpse of her.

As the chariots approached the entrance of the chateau, where both families were going to feast together in celebration of the wedding, many people wondered what would become of Mehsia if the prince married someone from outside the kingdom.

"There were so many ladies available within the royal court of Mehsia. And surely he could have chosen one of them," said Lady Futoma, a historian of the Kingdom of Mehsia. She had been serving the royal families by entertaining them with stories of the historical events of the kingdom, and rightfully so, because her opinion was held in high esteem within the royal court.

"Hmm, I didn't know he would choose a lady outside of Mehsia; strange, just utterly strange," replied Lady Marihn, a young maiden who served in waiting for Queen Jacuma. "I surely would have accepted his courtship," she said in playful and seductive manner.

"You are such a naughty little girl, but I adore it," said Lady Futoma. The two ladies looked at each other and began quietly laughing, using their fans to discreetly cover their smiles.

The trumpets sounded as the royal families approached the chateau. One royal chariot arrived immediately after the other.

"Isn't she a picture of pure beauty?" said King Ramnah proudly, as Princess Celina exited the chariot. The guardsmen escorted her through the courtyard into the chateau. They were followed by Countess Tierra and Lady Sari, each draped with royal fabric and beautiful gowns.

As Princess Celina and her party entered the chateau, Lady Sari was amazed at all the people and the beauty of the exquisite ancient décor. "How astonishingly beautiful this place is," she said looking around in wonderment.

"Utterly superlative," said Countess Tierra.

"Nice, but I am a little more fastidious than others," said Queen Mayora.

Princess Celina anxiously scanned the room and immediately set eyes upon Prince Kishan sitting in the middle of the long feasting table amid his parents and his court. She sighed in relief. She had thought maybe he would not show. But, she quickly dismissed those negative thoughts and replaced them with words of love. "He loves me," she mumbled to herself.

"Announcing, Princess Celina!" shouted the courtier as the trumpeters began to play. Every eye in the room moved quickly toward the front of the chateau to behold the beauty of Princess Celina. "How beautiful," the crowd murmured. The hundreds of guests stood in honor of Princess Celina. As she and her party gracefully walked down the red carpet aisle, decorated with yellow flowers, the Mehsia people bowed in her honor.

Prince Kishan stood up and walked over to greet the princess at the end of the aisle. She slowly approached him with love in her eyes. He took her hand, bowed, and led her back to the table where she would sit next to him.

"How adorable," said Queen Jacuma to King Hubaka.

"Yes, a splitting image of our engagement dinner many years ago," replied King Hubaka. They smiled in adoration of their son, Prince Kishan.

After the announcements and introductions of the dignitaries, the musicians begin playing and the guest chattered amongst themselves. Then suddenly, the trumpets sounded, and Lord Phillip stood to make a toast and officially announce the engagement of Prince Kishan to Princess Celina. "We have been brought together to celebrate the joining of two kingdoms in holy matrimony—to celebrate the engagement of someone dear to my heart, kind of a son to me, Prince Kishan!"

All the people in the room shouted, "Hooray! Hooray!"

Prince Kishan stood. "Thank you, Lord Phillip, for the introduction. But, I would be nothing without the love of my parents King Hubaka and Queen Jacuma."

"All hail!" shouted the people.

"Now, I would like to introduce my betrothed, Princess Celina, and her family," said Prince Kishan. He introduced King Ramnah and Queen Mayora, Countess Tierra, Lady Sari, and lastly Princess Celina.

"All hail!" shouted the crowd again.

Princess Kishan said, as was traditional, "I will parade my bride-to-be in a dance for lovers." He took Prince Celina by her hand and led her to the dance floor for a sensuous and provocative dance. The dance lasted for more than ten minutes as the couple twirled, swayed, swung, and entangled their bodies to the sounds of the music. Up to the very last beat the crowd waited in anticipation of their next move. The crowd "Woo"ed and "Aw"ed as the couple swept in and out of each other's arms, symbolizing romantic moves that portrayed their love for each other. It seemed as though they were in a trance, consumed by a spirit of eternal love.

As the music came to an end, so did the illusion of love on the dance floor. Prince Kishan seemed to be unmoved by the dance and a little confused by the feelings he was displaying while dancing.

He immediately grabbed Princess Celina by the waist and spun her in toward him as though he would give her the 'lover's kiss.' He starred intensely into her eyes as the whole room sat in suspense and silence. "Is he going to kiss her?" they wondered.

Countess Tierra held her breathe in anticipation of his next move. "Is he going to kiss her?" she thought. That would just shatter her dream and infatuation with the prince. "Maybe," she thought, "he does love Princess Celina."

Lady Zorresia thought, "Oh no, please no, Prince Kishan, don't do it. It is me you love, not her. I am supposed to be your wife."

Every young maiden in the room sat in anticipation of seeing if their hopes and dreams of marrying the prince would end and of how heartbroken they would feel if the prince were to kiss the princess in their presence.

But Prince Kishan hesitated. He knew this would be the time to end all and save his family. "Just kiss her, just do it now," he thought to himself. He slowly lifted his eyes toward the table and noticed a tear rolling down the face of Lady Sari. He could feel the sadness in her heart and could sense the pain he would cause her if he kissed Princess Celina at this critical moment.

As the crowed waited in great anticipation of the 'Lover's Kiss,' he slowly twirled the princess away from him with his hand around her waist. He motioned her to bow for the crowd and suddenly exited the dance floor, quickly returning to his seat.

Prince Celina was left alone in the middle of the dance floor. He couldn't do it, he didn't kiss her, and she was confused but mostly embarrassed by the prince's behavior. She disappointedly followed him and also quickly returned to the table.

Once seated, the crowd applauded the couple for the seductive, but unfinished lover's dance.

The trumpet sounded again. "Let us feast!" shouted the courtier. Everyone began to feast on the enormous display of food on the table. Centered on the table among a variety of breads, cheeses, fruits, and pastries, was a roasted wild boar with an apple stuffed in its mouth.

"That looks delightful," said Queen Jacuma breaking the silence at the royal table.

"Yes, I certainly agree," replied Queen Mayora.

"I could eat the whole damn head," laughed Ouray, as he joined the conversation between the two queens.

Queen Mayora leaned over and whispered, "No kiss. Is there trouble in paradise?"

"I think there maybe a little something, because last night—" As Countess Tierra began to recap the conversation that had taken place the night before between her and the princess, she was rudely interrupted by Lady Zorresia.

"What are you ladies whispering about?" asked Lady Zorresia.

"Oh, just admiring the beautiful feast," replied Countess Tierra. She smiled at Queen Mayora.

"Here, eat some berries. I'm quite sure you are famished," Queen Mayora said to Lady Zorresia.

"Well, I'll have a bit, but I must watch my waist. I have been indulging a little bit too much lately," replied Lady Zorresia as she grabbed the berries.

"A little bit!" laughed Princess Celina. "Oh Zorresia, you are humorous, aren't you?"

Embarrassed by the princess's comment regarding her weight, Lady Zorresia placed the cheese and berries back on the tray. "Excuse me, I have to freshen up," she said as she left the table.

"How mean of you," Countess Tierra said scornfully to Princess Celina. "I will go and comfort her." Countess Tierra followed Lady Zorresia into the ladies' parlor.

"How dare she treat me like some fat slob!" cried Lady Zorresia. "I went to great lengths to plan this event to please her and the prince on this special day. How ungrateful she is. I don't deserve this type of subordinate treatment."

"I know the words of my sister were hurtful.

Please forgive her," said Countess Tierra. "She is under immense pressure to please the prince. Here, wipe your eyes. You are ruining your makeup. Now, look at yourself in the mirror." The two ladies laughed at the smeared makeup running down Zorresia face.

"Oh! It's horrible," said Lady Zorresia.

Meanwhile, Princess Celina tried to show affections toward Prince Kishan during dinner, but he repeatedly rejected her. Under the table, she placed her hand on top of his hand. But he immediately pulled it away.

Prince Kishan was distant from the festivities. He was worried about how Lady Sari was feeling about the whole situation. He nervously wondered how much more her little heart could handle.

Anxious to gain the queen's attention, Lord

Phillip approached Queen Jacuma and asked her to dance. "Hello King Hubaka, might I trouble you and the queen? Might I ask the queen for a dance?"

"Of course, Lord Phillip, you are a great warrior for our kingdom," replied King Hubaka.

"Well, might I have a say in this discussion?" said the queen. "It is me he would like to dance with."

"Well, madam?" said Lord Phillip as he held out his hand to Queen Jacuma. Queen Jacuma accepted and placed her hand in his, and he led her to the center of the dance floor.

"You look lovely, My Queen," said Lord Phillip as he lustfully stared at the queen. His gaze began at the bust line of her gown which revealed just a glimpse of her full breast. He glanced along her neckline up to her beautifully defined facial features and finally rested upon her beautiful brown eyes. "How refreshing," he thought as he enjoyed his selfish desiring of the queen.

"If you keep staring at me like that, Lord Phillip, my husband will become very jealous and behead you," said the queen in an attempt to break Lord Phillip's intense obsession with her.

"I will try to contain myself, My Queen," replied Lord Phillip as he slowly embraced her while dancing.

Meanwhile, Countess Tierra and Lady Zorresia returned to the table in much better spirits.

"Thank you, Princess, for reminding me of my overindulgence in feasting," Lady Zorresia said apologetically to Princess Celina.

"Gladly," replied Princess Celina. "See she's grateful for my comments," she said to Prince Kishan.

Prince Kishan looked at Princess Celina in total

disgust. "You are so blinded by this mockery of an engagement and wedding, that can't see when you are causing hurt to others. Princess, you sadly disappoint me every waking day of my life."

Prince Celina was devastated by his words. Unable to speak, she sat in silence.

Lady Zorresia asked the princess if she would like her to freshen her drink.

"That would be fitting for you," replied the princess tersely.

Lady Zorresia picked up the princess's cup and, unnoticed, sprinkled some herbs into the cup, then poured the drink.

"Here, My Princess, a freshened cup of drink for you," said Lady Zorresia happily.

The princess took the cup and sipped the drink.

"Very refreshing," she said. "What is this drink?, ummm delicious. Tastes like berries and cream."

"Just freshly brewed", nervously replied Lady Zorresia. "Drink up, my princess. It is good for you."

CHAPTER 18

"What a great feast," said Queen Mayora politely.

"Yes, and well planned by Lady Zorresia," replied Queen Jacuma proudly. The two queens were cordial to one another despite the rumors of ill-feelings between them.

"We must keep in touch now that your son and my daughter will be married," said Queen Mayora.

"Yes, we should," replied Queen Jacuma nonchalantly. "My husband is searching for me and I must move along. Good day."

"Good day," said Queen Mayora.

The festivities were winding down, and the guests were getting a little bored. People were mingling and had made small talk with just about everyone in the room. Then suddenly, the trumpet sounded and everyone stopped to hear the announcements.

"King Hubaka will now present the dowry," said the courtier loudly.

"Now this is going to be very interesting, half-pint," said Ouray sarcastically as he nudged the shoulder of Casper who was sitting next to him.

"Don't ever touch me again, you immortal beast," said Casper sharply. He had never trusted or befriended

Ouray and, as a matter of fact, he totally despised the half-man, half-horse beast.

King Hubaka stood at the head of the table and said boisterously, "I present the following to the King and Queen of Isshi on my son's behalf for their daughter's hand in marriage. I present thee with 'the Golden Treasure.'"

During the entire dinner, King Ramnah had sat stony faced without engaging in any small talk except with Queen Mayora. But suddenly, a smile came upon his face. He was about to receive the gift he had been longing for.

King Hubaka summoned the servant to bring the golden box forward and present it to King Ramnah and his wife. The servant slowly walked toward the center of the table, where King Ramnah and Queen Mayora were sitting, and carefully placed the box in front of them. King Ramnah smirked in anticipation of the presentation of the Mehsia Medallion. The servant opened the box and inside was a row of gold coins. "I hereby offer you gold coins as the dowry for the princess." The crowd murmured with awe at the box of gold coins.

King Ramnah picked up the box of coins and examined them closely. He thought surely one of these coins must be the medallion. But since he had never seen the medallion, he was unsure. So he wisely slid the box towards the end of the table to Ouray and said, "Find it." All eyes in the room followed the box and rested on Ouray. The room was silent and everyone wondered what King Ramnah was searching for.

Ouray carefully examined each coin in the box, searching for the one with the magical powers of the medallion. He slowly turned to King Ramnah and shook his head. "It is not here."

King Ramnah stood up slowly from the table, looked around the room. With great vengeance and anger in his voice he asked, "Is this a joke? Have I been made a fool of? Where is the Medallion!" The entire room sat shocked at his bizarre actions.

King Hubaka was astonished. "I don't understand your request, King Ramnah," he said softly. And then he said changed the tone of his voice. "How ungrateful are you to reject my offering?"

Ouray started laughing loudly and applauded King Ramnah. Ouray stood and said, "You old fool of a king, speaking to King Hubaka. The dowry is not some foolish gold coins. That dowry is equal to the value of your life, old man!" He laughed again as he moved slowly toward King Hubaka. "I have sold your filthy life to King Ramnah," he said arrogantly. "You will die and Mehsia will be destroyed, if you don't present the Mehsia Medallion as the dowry!" Ouray walked grandiosely around the chateau.

The crowed screamed in shock and dismay. The once celebratory engagement dinner had now turned into a battle between two kingdoms. The crowd of dignitaries and courtiers, who had been dancing and celebrating together, was now about to be engaged in a bloody battle. Once again the historic lies and deceit that plagued these two powerful kingdoms many years ago had found their way back to the center of battle.

The guardsmen of the Isshi Kingdom pulled out their swords, as did the guardsmen of the Kingdom of Mehsia. Women and children who had been eating and playing together had taken sides. One woman from the kingdom of Mehsia immediately snatched a piece of meat out of the mouth of a young Isshi woman. "You won't eat anymore of our food!" yelled the Mehsian woman as she pushed the young lady of out the chair onto the floor.

Then a Mehsian man took the torch he was holding and set a fire the garment of an Isshi man. "How's that for wanting to steal our Medallion?" the man yelled. The Isshi man screamed in pain and ran over to the table and dashed a pitcher of water all over himself putting out the fire—but only after his skin was severely burned.

"Please hold on!" Prince Kishan shouted. "Let us explain."

"What is this nonsense regarding the Mehsia Medallion being offered as the dowry for the princess' hand in marriage?" asked King Hubbaka angrily.

"Good question, Father," Prince Kishan replied. "Why don't you ask your lovely wife that question?" He then turned and looked at his mother.

"Well," said Queen Jacuma hesitantly, "I have something to share with you, My King." She slowly walked toward him.

"Get on with the story, My Queen!" yelled Ouray. "Tell this feeble and worthless piece of garbage the deal that you made."

"That's enough, Ouray!" shouted the queen.

Casper quickly drew his sword and snarled at Ouray. "I can take him out, My Queen, just give me the word," he said viciously.

The tension between the guardsmen, the two kings, and the guests had risen to a bitter point of no return.

Queen Jacuma said, "I guess there is no easy way to say this. I promised the Medallion to King Ramnah to save the Mehsian army. We had lost the war," she cried, trying to win the sympathy of the people in the room and salvage her husband's respect.

"You are a liar. You are all liars!" suddenly yelled Lady Sari.

"Shut your mouth Sari! Let her continue," Queen Mayora said to Lady Sari. "Allow the queen to tell this intriguing story."

Prince Kishan looked over at Lady Sari with love in his eyes and hurt in his heart. He was saddened because he felt she was so young and innocent and wouldn't understand the hurtful secrets his mother was about to reveal.

Queen Mayora glanced around the room and

noticed Prince Kishan and Lady Sari staring at each other. "You bastard," she yelled. "She is only a young girl!"

Lady Sari quickly responded. "I'm no child, Mother. Do you think I don't know what you all have done? The lies, the secrets—it all disgusts me. I'm not that naïve. You all call yourselves royalty. Well everyone, the royal courts of both these kingdoms have been living a lie and have made a complete mockery and even bigger fools out of Princess Celina and Prince Kishan."

"Sari no, please stop don't say it," warned Queen Mayora. At this point, Queen Mayora realized that Lady Sari must have been the person outside the cave the night she'd told the kingdom secrets to Prince Kishan.

"Oh leave the young girl alone!" Ouray yelled. "Let her speak freely."

Lady Sari had the undivided attention of everyone in the room. "Father, I hate you for what you have done," she said. "You did this for what reason? Was it the power? I can't believe my own father would encourage his own daughter to marry her own brother—just to gain ultimate control of all the lands." Tears rolled down from Lady Sari's eyes. "How dreadful a man are you?" Everyone in the room sighed in disbelief and astonishment.

Prince Celina slowly walked over to her father in a state of disbelief. "Father, tell me this isn't true. Father, please tell Sari to take back those hideous words she spoke against you, me, and Prince Kishan. Look me in my face and tell me that is not true, Father. Father, answer me, please!" she cried.

King Ramnah did not reply. He just sat in silence and grew angry. He gritted his teeth and bitterly said to

Lady Sari, "Sit down, you little brat. You are just like your hateful mother."

Lady Sari continued to speak as though her father was invisible. "Yes princess, your fairytale prince is your brother. But most importantly, he doesn't love you. It is me whom he loves." Lady Sari ran to Prince Kishan and kissed him passionately on the lips.

Princess Celina looked at Prince Kishan and then quickly at Queen Jacuma. Feelings of betrayal overwhelmed her and she began to hysterically plead with her father to stop Lady Sari for telling these awful lies. She demanded that he behead anyone who repeated such madness.

"I'm afraid he can't stop her from telling the truth, my dear," confessed Queen Jacuma softly. "Yes, it is true. You are my daughter."

Princess Celina fainted and fell onto the floor, hitting her head. Countess Tierra and Lady Zorresia ran to her side.

King Hubaka turned to Queen Jacuma. "My Queen, what are you saying?"

"I'm sorry, my love,' Queen Jacuma replied. "I've never meant to hurt you."

King Hubaka stood. "I refuse to continue to break bread with you people. Lord Phillip, please prepare my carriage." He turned to Queen Jacuma and said, "I will speak with you in private regarding this matter."

"Yes, your Majesty," replied Lord Phillip.

"Wait one minute, you old bastard!" shouted Ouray. "There's more. I'll give you one guess as to who the princess' dad-tay is?" He fell into an uncontrollable state of laughter as he pointed at King Ramnah.

King Ramnah suddenly threw a dagger toward Ouray, missing Ouray's head but nipping him on the ear.

Blood began to drip down Ouray's face as he continued to laugh. He wiped the blood with his hand and tasted it. Then he laughed again.

King Hubaka fell to the floor, grabbing his heart. Queen Jacuma ran to this side and kneeled beside him. She yelled for Lord Phillip to hurry and fetch the carriage to take King Hubaka home to rest. Lord Phillip picked up the feeble king and placed him in the royal carriage.

Ouray continued his vengeful episodes of laughter, saying, "Die! Die! Hope you burn in hell."

In the blink of an eye, Casper leaped over the table with his sword, almost as though he were flying in the air, and cut off Ouray's head. Blood squirted everywhere, and the crowd screamed at the horrific sight.

Ouray's head fell and went rolling around on the floor. The crowd kicked the head around as if they were playing soccer. The half-man, half-horse's beheaded body frantically ran around the room in search of the head, finally locating it in the fireplace. Once the body and the head were united in the fire, a fiery image of Ouray emerged from the fireplace and shouted, "You have not seen the last of me. I will kill you all!"

King Ramnah went to Prince Kishan and grabbed him by the collar. "This does not change anything. You will marry my daughter as promised and deliver the Mehsia Medallion to me."

"I will do nothing of the sort and take your bloody hands off me. My father is the only person who knows where the Mehsia Medallion is hidden," replied Prince Kishan aggressively, pushing the king's hands away from his collar.

"Let him go!" Lady Sari yelled at her father.

"How dare you challenge me for this piece of shit? Take her away," said King Ramnah to his guardsmen.

"Let her go," yelled Prince Kishan as he tried to save Lady Sari. The guardsmen grabbed and restrained him, too.

King Ramnah moved closer toward Prince Kishan and said through gritted teeth, "You'd better hope that old bastard lives to tell you were the Medallion is hidden, or I will kill her." He pointed to Lady Sari.

"No, My King!" cried Queen Mayora. "I beg you—not my youngest daughter!"

"Tomorrow by noon, the Medallion must be in my possession, or she dies!" King Ramnah shouted at Prince Kishan.

CHAPTER 19

Sadness and solemnity lingered in the air. One could sense the morbidity lurking around the palace walls, seeking whom it might devour. The servants were quiet and cautious with their chores, while Prince Kishan sat nervously writing in his journals.

King Hubaka was lying nearly breathless on his bed. Queen Jacuma sat in sorrow and weeping by his side.

"I loved you, my dear," he whispered in her ear, "but there is a regret I have concerning you." He paused. "Why did you disgrace my family's name?" Tears rolled down his face. "He is our only son. How could you, Jacuma?" He wept with deep sorrow and humiliation.

"My love, my only love, I wanted to tell you so many times. But, I couldn't bring myself to tell you such terrible things about my past. It happened so long ago. I was a very young girl and well, I never meant to hurt you. Allow me to regain your love and trust. What can I do?" the queen desperately pleaded.

"Unfortunately I don't have enough time left for you to redeem yourself," replied the king.

"Then allow me to redeem my only son's love. My King, I have only one last request of you. Please tell me where the Mehsia Medallion is hidden. King Ramnah has threatened to kill Prince Kishan's true love—his own daughter, Lady Sari—if the Medallion is not delivered to him by noon tomorrow. Yes, I have shamed our family, but it will destroy Prince Kishan if she is harmed. I beg of you, there isn't much time to spare!" she pleaded.

King Hubaka stared into Queen Jacuma eyes. "I would like to see my son now."

Queen Jacuma hurried to the door and instructed the servants to summon the prince.

Shortly after, Prince Kishan entered the room and kneeled down next to his father's bed. "Yes, Father—you called?" he said.

"Yes, my son, I would like to speak with you in private," said the king in a soft, solemn whisper. King Hubaka told Prince Kishan to follow his heart and save his true love Lady Sari by turning over the Mehsia

Medallion to King Ramnah. He told his son about the story of how he followed his own heart and married Queen Jacuma against his parent's wishes. King Hubaka explained that years ago it had been rumored that the young maiden he had selected as his bride was not a virgin, but he hadn't cared because he loved her.

"I loved your mother," said King Hubaka. "I trusted her with everything I ever treasured. She holds my most prize possessions. I loved her with all my heart as you now love young Lady Sari with the same love and compassion. Follow your heart, my son, and take the Medallion. Give it unto King Ramnah."

"No, Father," replied the prince.

"Promise me, promise me this you will do, my son," King Hubaka desperately pleaded.

"I know not where the Medallion is, my father," said Prince Kishan.

217

King Hubaka replied, "If you examine your mother closely, you'll find the Mehsia Medallion."

Prince Kishan sat puzzled by his father's remarks and wished his father hadn't told him where to look for the Medallion. Prince Kishan kissed his father on the forehead and began to weep as King Hubaka fell into an eternal sleep, dying in his son's arms. "There is no greater honor to a young man," thought Prince Kishan, "than to experience holding his father during his last waking hours."

Prince Kishan could no longer hold his sorrow. He painfully yelled, "FATHER!" as he cried holding King Hubaka's lifeless body. The loud cry sent the servants running into the bedroom only to be met by the death of their king.

While still mourning his father's death, Prince Kishan desperately sought answers to the riddle of locating the Medallion and rescuing Lady Sari.

Queen Jacuma entered the room where King Hubaka's body lay and sadly said, "Our king has truly left us, hasn't he?" Then she suddenly asked, "Did he tell you where the Medallion is hidden?"

"No," replied Prince Kishan.

Queen Jacuma kneeled beside the king's deathbed in regret and sorrow. "I loved you with all my heart, My King," she whispered to his dead body, because his soul was long gone away.

"I will leave you to mourn alone," said the prince as he walked over to his mother. "I must find a way to save Lady Sari."

"How can you think of yourself during the death

of your father?" cried the queen angrily. Then suddenly and impulsively, she reached up and slapped Prince Kishan on the face.

Shocked, he grabbed his face and stared at her. Before he could speak he noticed that his face was bleeding. He grabbed his mother by the arm and looked at her hand. He noticed that her usual ring had caused the wound to his face.

He remembered the words of his dying father: *"Closely examine your mother and you will find the Mehsia Medallion."* Prince Kishan held her arm tightly as he carefully examined his mother.

"You are hurting me!" yelled Queen Jacuma as she struggled to loosen her arm from the prince's grasp.

But the prince was deep in thought. He noticed an unusual charm that hung around the queen's neck. He closely examined the charm and then suddenly snatched it from around the queen's neck and ran towards the door.

Queen Jacuma ran after him yelling, "Are you crazy? Your father gave that to me!" She grabbed the prince's cloak.

He pushed her aside and said. "Not now, Mother. I must save Sari."

CHAPTER 20

Lady Sari was still hanging in the palace dungeon. She had been badly beaten and assaulted by the guardsmen. King Ramnah sat in the parlor of the palace, waiting patiently for Prince Kishan to bring the Medallion.

As noontime approached, Queen Mayora and Countess Tierra entered the parlor. "Hello My King," said Queen Mayora.

"What brings you here?" replied the king aggressively. "How is Princess Celina?"

"She is coping just fine, My King," replied Queen Mayora.

"Good," said King Ramnah.

"My King, it is almost noon and I have come to beg for the life of my youngest child, Lady Sari. She's doesn't know any better, my lord. Please spare her life," pleaded Queen Mayora.

"I have heard enough. You may leave me now," replied the king.

"You bastard, how can you be so heartless to our daughter?" cried the queen.

"Take her away!" the king ordered his servants.

"Do not touch me. I am your queen," said Queen Mayora. But the servants obeyed the king's orders and dragged Queen Mayora away from his presence.

King Ramnah then went down to the dungeon

where Lady Sari was being held captive. "I guess your beloved prince isn't coming to rescue you," he said. "You turned your back on your own father for the love of a simple coward."

"He's no coward—he's more of a king than you are," she replied.

Upset by her words, King Ramnah walked over to Lady Sari and hit her in the face. "I am the king, and you shall not talk to me in that manner."

"You are not my father, you are not my king!" yelled Lady Sari bitterly as she spit on him.

Angered by her remarks, King Ramnah turned to his guardsmen. "Have your way with her; then maybe she will understand who I am." King Ramnah exited the dungeon and returned to the parlor.

The guardsmen walked over to Lady Sari and

fondled her breast, ripped off her clothing, and began to violently beat and rape her frail body. She cried out to Prince Kishan to save her, then cried to her mother to save her, then her cried to her sisters to save her until she had no more tears to cry. Her young feeble body was numb to the abuse. She finally passed out. Each guardsman took a turn raping and sodomizing young Lady Sari. After the first guardsman, Paul, had his way with her, he then resumed his post outside the palace and summoned the next guard to continue with the raping. One after the other, they violated her body.

During the dark night, Prince Kishan dismounted his horse within view of the palace of Isshi. Just barely missed by the guardsmen, Prince Kishan carefully approached the window that was slightly open near the palace dungeon. He got down on his knees and crawled closer to the window. As he slowly approached, he could hear the moans and grunts of men and the whimpering of a young lady. He prayed that Lady Sari was safe and without harm, but he knew deep down inside that his most terrifying fears were within moments of his sight. He tried to prepare himself before looking in the window, but nothing would have been sufficient for what he beheld—Barnabias raping poor Lady Sari.

Prince Kishan was crushed. He quickly sat beside the palace, gasping for air and vomiting as he witnessed the most grueling acts one man can perform on a woman, and not just any woman, but the little lady of his dreams. Barnabias was a savage, huge in stature with enormous hands and feet. Prince Kishan wiped the vomit from his mouth and prepared to behold the heinous sight again. He peeked through the window, but this time he could see

Lady Sari.

She was bent over and lying on the table almost lifeless and paralyzed as the three hundred pound animal of a man repeatedly entered in and out of her rectum, his penis forcing blood to flow. Barnabias was enjoying her petite body as he held her head in place with his strong forearm. Prince Kishan looked into her eyes and he could see that she had become indifferent to the pain.

"How could her father, King Ramnah, allow such heinous and lewd acts upon his own daughter?" the prince thought. "I must save her! The love of my life, my love," he whimpered softly as tears rolled down his face.

Lady Sari could see the prince from her view and she slightly responded to his hurt and pain and displayed her own. Prince Kishan could see the pain and humiliation in her eyes. He felt her eyes were pleading for him to save her from the lewd and vile acts.

Inspired by her pain, Prince Kishan took his bow and arrow from his back and positioned the arrow. He drew back the bow and released it. The arrow pierced Barnabias in the back of his head and exited through his forehead. Barnabias immediately stopped his stroking, and fell forward on top of her.

Lady Sari sighed in great relief and, with her remaining strength, pushed her brutal assailant onto the floor. In pain and bleeding from the sexual assaults, she slid off the table down onto the floor and began to weep. After a few moments, Lady Sari began to crawl toward the staircase into the main house.

Prince Kishan entered through the window, ran over to Sari, and tightly wrapped his arms around her.

With tears in his eyes, he said, "My love, my love, I'm sorry, I'm so sorry."

Lady Sari looked Prince Kishan in the eye and softly whispered, "I knew you would come for me." She then fainted in his arms.

Prince Kishan carried her up the staircase to the bedroom where Queen Mayora and Countess Tierra were praying. He quietly opened the door and laid Lady Sari's feeble and bruised body on the bed.

Queen Mayora immediately began to care for and nurture the wounds of her young daughter. Countess Tierra sat in disbelief and shock at the condition of the young girl's bruised and beaten body.

Queen Mayora cried as she wiped away the blood flowing from her vaginal area. "Don't just sit there, help me with her," she demanded.

Countess Tierra immediately fetched a pitcher, filled it with water, and slowly poured it over Lady Sari, who trembled in pain. The two women wept as they cleaned the wounds that covered the brutally battered body of the young girl.

CHAPTER 21

As King Ramnah sat lounging in his pride, he pondered his next move against Mehsia and Prince Kishan. It angered the arrogant king that the young prince had not delivered the Mehsia Medallion. He thought, "Will I order an attack of some sort, or will I just send soldiers to capture and kill the young prince and the royal family?"

"Father," a soft voice called out from afar. "Father," she softly said again.

"Yes?" he angrily replied. "I thought I told the guards that no one is to disturb me!" he yelled.

"It is I, Father," said Princess Celina softly.

"Oh, my dear daughter, I did not know it was you," said King Ramnah as he quickly changed his disposition and turned around to greet his daughter with open arms. Startled by her wayward appearance, King Ramnah hesitantly asked, "Did you get a good rest?

"Yes, Father," replied Prince Celina.

"Have a seat my dear, you look famished," said the king.

"No Father, I feel just fine," replied Princess Celina euphorically.

King Ramnah had not seen Princess Celina since the feast. He felt a sense of uneasiness about her. He could sense something different in his daughter's behavior. Unbeknownst to him, earlier that day during the engagement feast, Lady Zorresia had laced the princess's drink with opiates of ecstasy.

Prince Celina had an unusual eerie and demonic spirit that was also sensual and seductive. Her hair was wildly scattered atop her head, her eyes were piercing like those of a wild animal, and her skin was glazed with an unusual pale dusty white glow.

As King Ramnah closely observed his daughter, he noticed several creatures exuding from different parts of her body. One of the creatures crept out of her body, floating through the air toward the king, stopping just inches from his face. The creature attempted to seduce him by slowly licking the side of his face. Astonished, he grabbed the side of this face and swiftly shook his head in disbelief.

"Father, I do love you," said Princess Celina as she slowly approached him.

King Ramnah cautiously stepped back.

"Do you fear me, Father?" said Princess Celina as she glided closer toward him.

King Ramnah did not answer his daughter. He stood silently questioning whether or not the person standing before him, who looked and sounded like his precious daughter, was really his daughter.

"Don't be silly, Princess," replied the king. "I would never fear my own daughter."

Princess Celina slowly smiled.

Suddenly, a guardsman hastily enter the chambers and said, "Pardon my lord, I must interrupt."

"What is it?" said the king.

"Someone has murdered Barnabias."

"Murdered Barnabias?" shouted the king. "He's here," he thought. "Prince Kishan has returned." He asked, "Where is Lady Sari?"

"She has disappeared," replied the guardsman.

"How could this happen? You bumbling idiots. Go find them both and bring them to me," said King Ramnah angrily.

The guardsman rushed out of the chambers and began to gather up other men to search for Prince Kishan and Lady Sari.

"Let them go!" yelled Princess Celina to her father. "He loves Sari and he never loved me. At least one of us will be happy."

"I will do nothing of the sort," replied King Ramnah. "My own daughter has betrayed me, and I will make Princess Kishan and the kingdom of Mehsia pay for it."

"No, Father. You will pay for it," whispered Princess Celina softly. Suddenly, she seized her father's sword and plunged it into his heart. She then pulled the sword out of chest and used it to slit his throat. His blood splattered over her face. She wiped the blood from her face then placed her bloody fingers on her lips tasting her father's blood. Afterwards, she stood immobile, staring at her father's dead body. She horridly said, "Now, your blood truly runs in my veins and we will always be together, my true love. We are in eternal love, forever."

As Prince Kishan was making his getaway and swiftly dodging the guardsmen, he ran into the king's chambers, only to behold the horribly gruesome image of Princess Celina standing over King Ramnah's dead body, tasting his blood.

"Oh my God," he sighed. "No. No. What have you done, Princess?"

With glee in her eyes and a peaceful smile upon her face, Princess Celina turned to Prince Kishan. "I have just sanctioned my marriage to my true love, my father."

Countess Tierra approached the doorway and was astonished by what she saw: her sister was standing over her father's dead body, with his sword in her hand and blood dripping from her mouth. Countess Tierra became weakened by the bloody scene. She, too, sighed in disbelief. "Oh no, oh Princess no, please no. What have you done? What have you done!" she cried.

Startled by the screaming, Queen Mayora and the servants charged into the king's chambers, only to behold the same gruesome scene. Queen Mayora, overwhelmed by the sight of her lifeless husband on the floor, lying in a puddle of his own blood, felt sorrow for the man she had once loved. As she pushed her way through the guards to get a closer look at the deadly scene, she became weak at the knees and kneeled next to the king's body. "What a pitiful way to die for such a ferocious leader," she softly said. "He died at the hands of his own beloved daughter."

CHAPTER 22

Prince Kishan could sense the servants' unpleasant reaction to the slaying of King Ramnah. So, he slowly approached the queen and lifted her up by the arm and said, "We must go at once, My Queen."

The servants notified the guardsmen to immediately began to sound the trumpets to awaken the people and inform them that King Ramnah of Isshi had been murdered.

The people of the kingdom of Isshi responded with outrage and despair. They demanded answers. And when none were provided, they vandalized the palace, set fires in the towns, and chanted obscenities throughout the kingdom.

Prince Kishan forcibly commanded the ladies, "We must leave now." He instructed Countess Tierra and the queen to gather their treasures and meet him behind the palace. "Hurry," he demanded. "I will gather the horses and search for Lady Sari." He ran out of the room.

Countess Tierra frantically searched the room for the king's treasures.

"It's over there," said Queen Mayora pointing toward a lantern on the wall. "Turn the lantern and it will open a secret passageway."

Countess Tierra tried to turn the lantern but she didn't have enough strength. "Please Mother, come over here and help me!" she frantically yelled, as she could sense the crowd outside the palace becoming more and more violent.

The two ladies put their strength together and slowly turned the lantern, opening a small passageway.

"Hurry, inside," said Queen Mayora, pointing to the passageway beyond the wall. "There you will find a small treasure chest."

Countess Tierra slowly crawled inside the small passageway, waving her hands about searching for the treasure chest. It was very dark and Queen Mayora waited in suspense as Countess Tierra searched.

"Do you see anything? Have you found it?" said the queen impatiently.

Countess Tierra did not answer her.

"Tierra can you hear me?" asked the queen as she stooped down to get a closer look inside the small passageway. "Where are you?" she shouted.

Suddenly, one of the guardsmen grabbed the queen from behind and said, "Here she is—the filthy murderer."

"I'm not a murderer!" cried the queen, as she struggled to get away from the guardsmen.

"Let's burn this bitch and her little daughters," said another guardsman.

"Let me go, you bastard!" shouted the queen. She slammed the lantern over the guards' heads and they both fell onto the floor. The other guardsman drew his sword to strike the queen and suddenly he stopped, as though suspended in mid air, and fell to the floor.

An anonymous man had stabbed the guard in the back with his sword.

"Thank you," said the queen to the small statured man.

"You can thank me later. For now, we must hurry," said the man.

"Hold on, I must get my daughter!" yelled the queen. She crawled into passageway to search for Countess Tierra.

Suddenly, a voice said, "I got it, Mother." Countess Tierra had found the treasure chest and hurried out of the small passageway.

"Please ladies, we must go now before it's too late," said the small man. He could hear the angry voices of the guardsmen who were just steps away from the doorway. The three of them began to head toward the doorway, hoping to escape past the guardsmen.

"No, this way," says Queen Mayora. "The guardsmen are too close. The only way out is through the secret passageway. Get your damn sister, too," she yelled to Countess Tierra.

Countess Tierra pulled Princess Celina by the arm and all three of them entered the passageway.

"Ladies first," said the small man.

Crawling on their knees in the dark for over twenty minutes, they found their way to a small shutter opening in the rear of the palace.

First, Countess Tierra exited, followed by Queen Mayora, and then Princess Celina. Finally, the small statured man exited through the shutter, where they were met by Prince Kishan who was mounted on his horse with Lady Sari.

"What are you doing here?" the prince asked the small man, surprised.

"Your mother informed me of what you were up to, and I promised her that I would bring you safely back to Mehsia," replied Casper.

"I'm glad you are here," said Prince Kishan.

The two men embraced each other and then immediately assisted the women with mounting the horses. Prince Kishan, Lady Sari, and Countess Tierra mounted one horse. Casper, with Queen Mayora and Princess Celina, mounted the other horse. The entourage began their journey to back to Mehsia.

While riding, Princess Celina looked back at the crowd of people charging toward them, ranting and raging with anger, carrying torches in their hands and yelling, "Bloody murderers!"

Prince Kishan yelled, "Charge!" and kicked his horse into full gallop, while Lady Sari intensely held on to his waist.

During the ride to Mehsia, Princess Celina seemed a little melancholy. She was slowly awakening from her morbid state of mind as she envisioned her father lying dead, his body burned in the flames that had ignited within the palace. Her thoughts overwhelmed her, taking her back to the very first time she had announced her courtship to Prince Kishan. She clearly remembered that day and how her father had slapped her mother and verbally scorned Lady Sari. But what haunted her most about that day were the words of her sister, Countess Tierra. The countess had painstakingly pointed out to Princess Celina how gullible and naive she was regarding marriage and being in love.

Now, Princess Celina knew that her sister had been right. She knew nothing about real love or marriage. During her courtship with the prince, she had acted selfishly and had fallen prey to the fairytale of being in love.

"Brokenhearted, in a deadly and bloody mist of confusion," she thought. Feelings of disappointment and hurt overtook her as she realized that her youngest sister, Lady Sari, knew the true meaning of love, while she could only desire it. As she rode in silence, she thought, "How could a once hopeful and cheery fairytale turn into a horrendous nightmare filled with lost hopes and shattered dreams?"

As the entourage approached the hilltop overlooking Mehsia, a sense of relief fell upon the weary travelers. From the hilltop, they could see the town's people cheering and celebrating. The news, that Prince Kishan had saved the kingdom and King Ramnah was dead had reached Mehsia. Encouraged by the cheering and chanting of his name, Prince Kishan stiffened his posture and proudly led his small entourage down the hill top and safely home.

Prince Kishan carried Lady Sari into the palace and laid her feeble body on the bed in one of the guest chambers.

"Take good care of her," he told the servant.

"Who is she?," whispered the servant.

"She is someone special and dear to me," replied the prince.

"She's been beaten and raped, sir. What beast would do such a thing to this precious girl?," asked the servant.

"Please don't tell anyone. You must keep this a secret. Absolutely, no one must know, including the queen," said the prince.

"Your secret is safe with me. I will tell no one," replied the servant.

The prince was tired from the long travel and wanted nothing more than to rest. But he knew that he had to hide Queen Mayora and Countess Tierra from his mother. He knew that his mother would be upset with him once she discovered that he had brought King Ramnah's family to live in Mehsia.

"My Lord, which room shall I prepare for the other guests?," asked the servant.

"Uh, they won't be residing here. I will take them to a friend's home for resting," replied the prince.

"I'm very tired and would like to rest," said Queen.

"Just a little while longer of traveling," said the prince.

"What do you mean, more traveling?, shouted the Queen.

"Queen, please lower your voice. You will awaken the whole palace."

"Can't you see mother, we are not welcome here. The prince is only concerned with his precious little Sari," said Countess Tierra.

"No, that is not true. It's just that I need to discuss with mother that you will be staying in Mehsia."

"You are king, now my prince," said Casper. "Surely, you can make this decision without the approval of your mother."

"I guess you are right! I am the king and I am the ruler of this kingdom."

"Ruler, my ass. Until we have the Official ceremony, I am in charge of this kingdom," said Queen Jacuma. "What is going on and why are these people in my palace?, she asked.

Prince Kishan was shocked to see his mother standing in the doorway. He knew from the tone in her voice that she was not happy to see his new guests.

EPILOGUE

I hope you enjoyed the numinous beginnings of Mehsia's Medallion. As Prince Kishan returns home to lead the kingdom, as the new king, he and his friends will encounter new intriguing challenges and adventures.